W9-DAO-716
3 4028 09402 8918
HARRIS COUNTY PUBLIC LIBRARY

JUPITER STORM

MARTI DUMAS

Illustrations by Stephanie Parcus. Published by Plum Street Press, New Orleans, LA, USA.

ISBN: 978-1-943169-34-4
JUV037000 JUV FICTION / Fantasy & Magic
JUV012030 JUV FICTION / Fairy Tales & Folklore
JUV014000 JUV FICTION / Girls & Women

For my mother. Her memory is here.

CONTENTS

1
JACKIE

Jacquelyn Marie Johnson was exactly the kind of girl she should be. Tiny, talkative, and sharp as a tack. She liked paper dolls and long division and imagining things she had never seen. But most of all Jackie liked being in charge. And that was a good thing because she was also really good at it.

The students in Jackie's school were the most well-educated assortment of toys on the planet. They knew all of Aesop's fables and the tales of Compere Lapin in English and French, their mul-

tiplication facts through nine, the difference between area and perimeter, and, in theory, how to make shrimp and redfish stew. None of the toys were allowed to use the stove, of course, but they could recite the recipe and preparation techniques by heart.

Without Jackie's guidance, the toys would have been a truly unruly lot. This was also the case for her brothers. There were five of them—Jacob, John, Jonah, Judah, and Sam. Jackie wasn't the oldest, and she wasn't the biggest, but she was the most in charge.

Jackie's mother knew she needed to be in charge of things. Important things. So she gave Jackie important responsibilities. For example, Jackie was in charge of watering the plants. Jackie was in charge of adding things to the grocery list. And every afternoon Jackie was in charge of getting all five of her brothers to come inside for dinner. This was the hardest job of all, but it wasn't hard for Jackie. Even though her brothers were all over the neighborhood doing all kinds of things, all she need-

ed to get them inside was a metal pot, a wooden spoon, and a stern look.

She would clang the pot three times, call each boy by name, then clang the pot once more—for emphasis. The boys would come running when they heard her signal, but just in case any of them had a mind to be sassy with her about how the street lights were not on yet and it was too early to come in, after she had finished banging on it, Jackie would put the pot on the porch bottom side up and step up on it like it was a stage or a throne, her perfectly polished Mary Janes glinting in the early evening light.

Standing on the pot, Jackie was tall enough to use her stern look to stare away all the excuses and the reasons why, so that all five brothers washed their hands at the hose outside and filed into the house as quiet and orderly as a communion line.

The neighbors marveled at her. Some of them laughed, but it was only the laugh people do sometimes when they are pleasantly surprised.

Who could blame them? It was impressive to see someone so little commanding such authority, even when you have seen it many, many times before.

So on this particular day after the neighbors had gathered to watch Jackie send her brothers inside, they were too busy smiling with each other and chuckling knowingly about Jackie's little ribbons and her shiny little shoes to notice when Jackie noticed the egg.

2
THE CHRYSALEGG

As the screen door snapped to a shut behind her last brother, Jackie grabbed the spray bottle from its hook and mentally prepared herself to leave the porch. It was time to do battle with the aphids.

Aphids were a tough business. They poked tiny holes in plants and sucked the plant's food out before the plant had had a chance to eat it, which Jackie thought was extremely rude. She also didn't like the way sad, aphid-eaten leaves looked mixed into her perfect, cheerful garden. So, every

evening after she sent her brothers inside, she checked the leaves for aphids and squirted as many of them off as she could before she went inside herself.

It would have been nice to have her brothers' help. She had even almost asked them once. But then a vision of them galloping through the garden, crushing petals and ripping off leaves like mad-men stopped her from making that mistake. She could do it herself. Her shoes got dirty, but she didn't mind. Lavender mary janes were beautiful, even caked with mud. And every time she cleaned them off before going back into the house she felt like an archaeologist uncovering a lost treasure.

Spray bottle in hand, she took stock of the land-scape before leaving the porch. The hose wasn't dripping, so Jacob, the last brother to wash his hands, must have done a good job tightening it. Wrinkling her nose, she realized she could see a few aphids from where she was standing high on the porch. That wasn't a good sign. If they were

visible from that far away, there must have been hundreds more that she couldn't see, poised to poke holes and suck the life out of every plant in her care. Not if she could help it.

Her mother did not allow her to spray the garden with chemicals, but a spray bottle of water with a drop of dish soap and a lot of determination were all the weapons she needed. Generalissima Jackie mentally prepared herself to launch the first wave of attack, but when she turned to charge down the stairs and into the garden, a tiny glint of orange in one of her flower pots caught her eye.

Jackie had three flower pots. She kept them separate from the rest of the garden, hidden in a nook at the base of the steps. Not that she was ashamed of them. Never that. But the flower pots contained snapdragons and, being from up north, snapdragons were too delicate to survive the New Orleans sun. At least that's what her aunt had said in the note that arrived with the package.

Dearest Jacquelyn,
Your mother tells me you like to be in charge of things.
That is wonderful! I like to be in charge of things, too and,
what's more, I'm very good at it.
I look forward to seeing you see you again.
meantime I am sending you something to
enclosed are snapdragon seeds. They
here and are quite beautiful. I would
full grown when I visit, and I am
garden. I hope you will take very
Sincerely,
Your Great Aunt Mamie Seal
P.S. Take care that they do
just right amount should
Mount Hood,
Oregon

Dearest Jacquelyn,

Your mother tells me you like to be in charge of things. That is wonderful! I like to be in charge of things, too and, what's more, I'm very good at it.

I look forward to seeing you again, but in the meantime, I am sending you something to take charge of. The enclosed are snapdragon seeds. They grow freely on the mountain here and are quite beautiful. I would very much like to see them full grown when I visit, and I am told you are in charge of the garden. I hope you will take very good care of them.

Sincerely,
Your Great Aunt Mamie Seal

P.S. Take care that they do not receive too much sun. A just right amount should suffice.

Instead of planting them straight into the ground, Jackie asked her mother for some pots to plant them in. That way she could move them if they weren't happy. Eventually, her snapdragons found a home they liked at the base of the steps leading up to her front porch. There they got the softest, gentlest morning light but were shaded for the rest of the day. They were across a walkway from the other flowers, so they hadn't been invaded by the aphids—yet. So when a tiny glint of orange from one of the flowerpots caught Jackie's atten-

tion, Jackie feared the worst. If the aphids had crossed the great divide and invaded her snapdragon pots, her Great Aunt Mamie would be so disappointed.

She bounded down the stairs, her lavender shoes clicking with each step. If the aphids had made it to the pots, she would deal with them immediately, with her bare hands if necessary. But on closer inspection, she found that her worry had been in vain. There were no aphids in any of the flower pots. Not a one. So what had she seen, then? She spent the next several minutes turning over each leaf as gingerly as she could, carefully inspecting each one. She didn't find any aphids, but she did find what had caught her attention.

It was an egg, or at least she thought it was. Among the green leaves, the little egg hardly should have stood out at all, but it did. It was pale green like a monarch chrysalis but much too round. On closer inspection, it did look very much like a monarch chrysalis, right down to the delicate lines overlapping each other like tiles on a roof and the way it

dangled attached to the underside of a leaf. If it weren't for the tiny spot of orange near the top, she might not have seen it at all.

Was it an egg or a chrysalis? One thing was certain. She had never seen anything like it, and Jackie knew she needed to know more.

She stood up suddenly from where she had been squatting in front of the snapdragons. The little chrysalis egg had captured her attention, but her mother was probably wondering where she was by now. Jackie never took this long spritzing aphids in the evening. She dashed up the porch, wiped her shoes off with a towel hidden in the rocking chair cushions, and went inside.

Her brothers were already seated at the table looking far more angelic than they really were. The table had been set, the drinks had been poured, and her father was placing the last two bowls of red beans and rice on the table.

"Jackie's late," Jonah said smirking as Jackie sped to her place.

Leave it to Jonah to try to get her in trouble.

"Thanks, Captain Obvious," John replied. He said it quietly under his breath like he said most things, but it was loud enough for Jackie to hear as she sat down next to him.

Jackie smirked right back at Jonah in response. But with at least one other person on her side, Jackie's was the superior smirk.

Mama didn't say anything. When their father sat down, everyone joined hands. It was Sam's turn to say grace.

"Thank you for this food. Amen." Being the youngest, when Sam said grace it was both the cutest and the shortest.

After murmuring their amens, Mama passed around a basket filled with squares of cornbread. Everything seemed normal and pleasant until

Mama said, "So, why did it take you so long to come inside, Jacquelyn Marie?" Her mother always called her Jacquelyn Marie.

Jackie froze for a moment. She wanted to tell her mother about her discovery in the garden. Truly she did. What she didn't want was for Jonah or Jacob or one of the other ruffians to race outside and destroy the egg or chrysalis or whatever it was before she even had a chance to figure it out. Besides. They were her flowers, given to her personally by Great Aunt Mamie Seal, that she had grown from seed in the garden that she was in charge of. Nobody had a right to go invading and destroying any part of it. Not the aphids and definitely not one of her stupid brothers.

"I thought I saw an aphid in the snapdragons," she said.

"I thought I saw an aphid in the snapdragons," Jonah mouthed silently. He didn't dare mock her aloud with their parents at the table. Jackie shot him a look.

"But I didn't see any when I looked up close. I looked under every leaf just to be sure. That's what took so long." There. Her mother seemed satisfied. And everything she had said had been true. Technically. She hadn't lied, she just left a bit out.

The conversation continued with everyone sharing the best and worst parts of their day. Jacob had managed to get two desserts at lunchtime. One of John's drawings had gotten an honorable mention in an art contest. Jonah and Judah were Ace and King at foursquare for their entire recess, and Sam had been the line leader. Jackie hardly heard any of it. She couldn't get the image of the chrysalegg out of her mind.

3
FIRST CONFESSION

After dinner, when Jacob and John were finishing their homework and her father was helping Jonah and Judah get ready for bed, Jackie went to find her mother. She was in Sam and John's room rocking Sam to sleep. Even though Sam was already five, he was still the baby, and Mama still liked to rock him to sleep. Jackie sat quietly on the floor, lulled by the rhythm of the rocker, careful not to make a sound until Mama had settled Sam's sleeping form under the covers and they had both tiptoed out of

his room. Mama first put a finger to her lips, then silently motioned toward Jackie's room next door.

Jackie went in first, breathing a sigh of relief. There was always something comforting about walking into her own room and being surrounded by her own things. She so often had to share, but the bookshelves, the terrarium, the toy animals sitting in neat rows—they were all hers, and she didn't have to share them with anybody. Jacob, Jonah, and Judah all shared a room with two sets of bunk beds. John and Sam shared a room now, too, ever since Sam started sleeping through the night. But since she was the only girl, Jackie had a room all to herself, and she loved it that way.

Mama sat down on Jackie's bed and motioned for Jackie to sit next to her.

"What's wrong, Jacquelyn Marie?" her mother said. "Is something bothering you?"

Jackie blushed, suddenly embarrassed by her not-quite-a-lie at dinner. Mama hugged her a bit closer. It felt good.

"I wanted to ask you something," Jackie said.

"I figured as much," Mama smiled, "otherwise you wouldn't have come tipping into Sam's room looking for me. So, what is it?"

"I wanted to ask you if I can bring the snapdragons inside." She was really thinking of the chrysalegg but thought it best not to lead with that.

Mama looked skeptical. She didn't like dirt in the house. Not even potted dirt.

"Well, not all of the snapdragons," Jackie burst in, trying to talk long enough for her mother to think before she said no. "I'll be really neat, and I'll clean up any mess before you ever see it. Just one pot. The other ones can stay outside." She paused, but when her mother still didn't respond, she added, "It's...for science. I want to do an experiment to see if they will grow better outside or inside. For

school." She hadn't meant for that to happen. She hadn't meant for her not-quite-a-lie to turn into an actual lie, but it had. They did have to do a science project soon, but it was supposed to be about a favorite animal. If she hurried up and took it back, Mama might not even say anything.

Or maybe she would.

Or maybe she'd think that if Jackie were lying about something silly like a flower pot she might be lying about something bigger and therefore could never be trusted ever again. Jackie's heart beat a little faster.

Maybe if Jackie's mother knew that Jackie regretted the lie enough to take it back quickly, she might trust her even more, thinking that she had learned some sort of life lesson or something. Grown-ups were unpredictable like that.

The lie probably wasn't worth it. Jackie had all but decided to tell her mother the truth, when her mother said, "Okay, Jacquelyn Marie. If it's for sci-

ence. I trust you. Bring the flower pot inside, and don't go traipsing garden dirt in the house for it to get ground in my carpets."

It was too late. Her mother had spoken first. If Jackie took her words back now, it just wouldn't be the same. Would it? Jackie just said, "I will, Mama. Thank you."

Jackie's mother kissed her on the forehead. "And one more thing. If you see any little creatures in that pot, knock them off BEFORE you bring it inside."

Creatures? Did her mother just mention creatures? Jackie could practically feel the window of opportunity closing. This was her chance!

"Ok, Mama. I'll make sure there are no lizards on it." Her mother hated geckos and lizards even more than she hated dirt. "But do I have to knock them all off?" she added tentatively. "One of them has a chrysalis or an egg or something in it, and I

thought it would be fun to watch it while I do the experiment with the sunlight. For science."

"Oh, that's not a good idea, baby," her mother said. "If you're doing an experiment then the only thing that should be different is the thing you're testing for. Didn't your teacher teach you about too many variables in an experiment? Let me see the assignment sheet."

It was too soon for Miss Soraparu to have given them an assignment sheet for their animal project. It was on their big calendar, but it was more than a month away, and they had barely started talking about it. "There isn't one," Jackie covered quickly. "It's extra credit."

Instead of looking at her sideways, her mother kept going about the science. "Well, an experiment is a test to see if you can prove why something happens. So, if there is more than one something happening at the same time, you won't know which something made the change. Do all of the plants have eggs on them?"

"No. Just the one." Jackie's mind raced furiously for a way to turn this around. She did know about variables and collecting data, but she didn't think that now was the time to point that out, as much as she wanted to.

"Good. Then leave the one with the egg outside. Eggs hatch. Science or no science, I don't want whatever hatches from that egg crawling around my house," her mother laughed. "You can bring in the one with no egg and compare it with the other one with no egg outside. That way you'll only have one variable. It's better. Trust me."

"But..." Jackie hesitated.

"There's always a but, Jacquelyn Marie" her mother sighed. "Tell me why you can't just leave the infested one outside?"

Why couldn't she just leave it outside? It wasn't as if she didn't go outside every day. Was this one of those times when saying, "But it won't be the same!" would actually work? That had worked

when she caught that gecko. Her mother had let her keep it inside for two weeks, feeding it live crickets from a pet food store. That is until Jackie accidentally poured a few of the live crickets onto the floor instead of into the terrarium. They were able to catch two of them, but after that, her mother had calmly made her release the gecko back into the wild despite John's suggestion that they let it loose in the house to find the remaining crickets. Jackie still had the terrarium.

Truthfully, Jackie didn't know why she wanted to bring the chrysalegg inside so badly, but she did. She wanted to be able to watch it up close. It felt... important for some reason.

There was a loud thump from Jacob, Jonah, and Judah's room. This was not unusual, but it did catch her mother's attention.

Now or never, Jackie thought, *before the Js get her*. Jackie took a deep breath and poured out the whole story—being distracted from the aphids in the big garden, double-checking the hose was

turned off, hunting for aphids in the snapdragon pots, and being so mesmerized by chrysalegg that she was almost late for dinner. And since Mama was listening so attentively and already knew about Jackie's love for making strange, hybrid words, she never even had to ask Jackie what a chrysalegg was.

After a moment's pause, Jackie's mother stood and pulled her to her feet. "There's only one thing we can do now," she said, looking at Jackie intensely. Jackie felt a bit nervous. "Investigate," her mother finished with a smile, pulling Jackie outside. They didn't even stop to put shoes on.

Jackie's mother seemed almost disappointed after they had brought the snapdragon inside. They set it up on Jackie's desk next to her lamp.

"It's just a monarch chrysalis," her mother said. "Sometimes monarch caterpillars end up off course and form their chrysalises in odd places.

That might be why this one is so... malformed. It probably strayed away from the milkweed in the backyard, and now it's suffering for it."

Thanks to that patch of milkweed in their back-yard, Jackie had had the opportunity to observe lots of monarch caterpillars and chrysalises. Her mother was right. It didn't always work out. Some-times they climbed up to a high spot, formed a J and were stuck like that. Sometimes the chrys-alis formed, but a transformed butterfly never emerged. Sometimes the whole process seemed to work fine, but the butterfly that came out nev-er flew. She had seen lots of things go wrong, but never anything like this.

Her mother tsked. "Do you see that orange spot? Another malformation. It doesn't look good, baby. I doubt this butterfly is going to survive. You're just like my cousin Doll, always wanting to bring some half-dead thing inside. Are you sure you want to keep it in here?"

Jackie started to argue. She started to point out that maybe it wasn't a monarch chrysalis at all. Maybe it was another kind of butterfly, something neither of them had ever seen before. But then she thought better of it.

"Can I just watch it and see what happens? I've never gotten to watch it up close like this before."

"Okay," her mother sighed again. "But when it turns black and starts rotting you had better take it straight outside. I don't want any creatures decomposing in this house. Understand?"

"I understand. But..."

"But...? Jacquelyn Marie, why is there always a but?"

"But is it okay if we don't tell the Js?" she asked. "And Sam," she threw in, remembering that even though she lumped him in with the rest of the Js, Sam's name actually started with an S. "They'll mess around and hurt it even more."

"Are you going to take that thing outside the moment it hatches or starts turning black?"

"I will, Mama. I promise."

"Fine. I'll make sure your brothers stay out of your room." Mama got up to leave, shaking her head slightly. "And for the record, YOU are one of the Js," mama said before pulling Jackie's door closed. She didn't shut it all the way. Jackie's mother didn't believe in closed doors. But she did close it up enough for Jackie to have some privacy as she got ready for bed.

Jackie wasn't ready to get ready for bed, though. As soon as her mother left, she took out her drawing pad and colored pencils and began to sketch the chrysalegg. It felt good to sit so close to it. Like her whole body had been tense, but she could finally relax. In the light of her desk lamp, the orange spot looked more like a deep red. Like the storm on planet Jupiter. When she was done sketching she carefully wrote the date and "Day 1" at the

bottom of the page before putting away her drawing things and getting ready for bed.

That night she dreamed of flying.

4
PAPER FLOWER POTS

Jackie's mother needn't have been concerned about the mess Jackie's flower pot would make. What she should have been concerned with was tardiness. When you're a family of eight the tiniest bit of tardiness can snowball into a catastrophe, particularly in the morning. The morning routine in the Johnson household was an exact science. Like baking a cake, all the ingredients had to be measured just right, added in order, not over-

mixed or under-mixed, and baked at the perfect temperature for just the right amount of time.

If everything went according to plan, everyone's dishes were washed, and the entire clan besides her father would be loaded into the van and backing out of the driveway at 7:52.

Let Sam eat breakfast after he got dressed for school and he was sure to get blueberry stains all over his white shirt which meant he'd need to change and wouldn't be in the room to hear the reminder to pick up his lunch box and would make it half way to school with no lunch and no lunch which meant the whole operation had to turn around so the baby wouldn't starve before dinner.

Let Jonah and Judah wake up at the same time, and neither of them would take their turn in the bathroom because both would be too busy reenacting wrestling matches neither of them had ever seen. Jacob and John were no better. Jacob had to be awakened after Jonah and Judah had made

it to the breakfast table because, even though he was the oldest, he loved nothing more than goading his twin brothers into a good wrestling reenactment, and if John didn't get up early enough to play at least one round of animal cards with Sam and finish drawing whatever he had dreamed about, both he and Sam were unfit to be around other people.

Being a master chef, Jackie had several important jobs in the Johnson family morning routine, so when she lingered just a little too long over how much deeper and more beautiful the snapdragon petals were in the light of her room than they had been outside, it set off a chain reaction that resulted in their leaving a full ten minutes late. The morning routine was such an intricate production that no one knew for sure what had happened to make everything go so wrong. Jackie knew, but she was afraid to say so. Her mother was already obviously annoyed. When Jackie's mother was in a good mood, there was no better mother in the

universe. When she wasn't, it was best to watch yourself.

"I don't know what happened this morning," Jackie's mother said as she backed out of their driveway, "but if Mrs. Albertine is already on her front porch, we are even later than I realized."

Everyone in the van had the good sense to say, "Yes, Mama," even though their mother hadn't asked a question. They knew they all stood accused and that this wasn't a time to go to bat for themselves. Jackie knew that she was the one at fault, but she couldn't help noticing that their across the street neighbor, Mrs. Albertine, looked like she had been drinking coffee and reading the newspaper for quite a while. They couldn't be that late. She must have come out earlier than usual. Jackie desperately wanted to say so. What's the point of noticing things if you can't point them out? But somehow she managed to contain herself until their van pulled up to the school.

They weren't the last ones to arrive, which was a good sign, but Jacob used being "late" as an excuse to get to race through the building. Not to be beaten, Judah and Jonah followed suit. John didn't bother with actual running, but he did move his elbows back and forth a little faster. For her part, Jackie walked Sam to his classroom at a brisk pace, then she took the risk of running up the stairs to her classroom on the third floor. School was one of Jackie's favorite places to be, and she wouldn't have wanted to be late even if her teacher didn't let them play paper dolls before class started.

Jackie and her friend Ashley were the first to start the portable dollhouse folder thing. Their teacher, Miss Soraparu, seemed skeptical at first, but not for long. Relative to other fifth grade teachers, Miss Soraparu was only strict about a few things. There was no fooling around during fire drills, absolutely no talking or unnecessary movement during spelling tests, and the paper doll folders had to be completely put away by the time the bell rang, not to reappear until they lined up for

lunch or occasionally at the end of the day. Once the other kids figured out that Miss Soraparu didn't get angry about paper dingles on the floor or stray crayon marks on desks, the paper doll making had begun in earnest. Now pretty much every kid in the class had a folder of paper dolls and accessories—everything from little girls with unicorns to gruesome alien invaders—kept in a setting that was made out of the folder itself.

Jackie's own paper doll folder was a practical mix of characters from books she had read, fearsome beasts, and dress-up clothes. She wanted to draw some pots of snapdragons to add to the mix, but by the time she made it to her desk, everyone else was putting their paper doll folders away. She quickly unpacked, carefully placing her yellow paper doll folder on top of the left side stack in her desk before grabbing her writer's notebook and going to the rug for their morning literacy activity.

Jackie sat on the rug, crisscross applesauce with her notebook open in her lap. Then something really strange happened: Jackie didn't pay attention.

It's not that she wasn't thinking. She was thinking, just not about what Miss Soraparu was saying. She was thinking about her snapdragons.

Instead of writing whatever they were supposed to be writing about, Jackie wrote her predictions about how fast the snapdragons would grow. When Jackie's partner asked her a question, she couldn't answer right away. She had been thinking, scientifically, about whether it would be better to keep drawing the chrysalegg every day or to take a picture of it. A photograph would be more accurate, but Jackie didn't have a camera of her own and getting one might mean having to ask Jacob to borrow his. Camera or not, bringing Jacob into the picture was out of the question. It was probably better to be consistent anyway. She had drawn the night before. She'd keep drawing.

That's when Jackie noticed that her partner, Alex, had his hand up. She hated getting paired with Alex. He was always fooling around and never knew what they were supposed to be doing. He was probably about to ask to go to the bathroom

or something. But something told Jackie that Alex's hand wasn't about the bathroom. It was about her.

"Wait," she said, hoping to stop Alex from calling Miss Soraparu over.

"I need a new partner. You just fooling around. I gotta pass this quarter or I'ma have to repeat the fifth."

Alex was accusing her of fooling around? That was rich. Alex was the king of fooling around. Jackie mentally rewound their conversation, calling up the last thing Alex said.

"You said you want to pick something poisonous." Rapid recall skills came in handy. "You don't want to look in the mammals, then. There aren't too many poisonous mammals. Stick to insects or reptiles."

"Alright," Alex said, putting his hand down before Miss Soraparu came over. He sounded skeptical, but he started flipping pages in their science

book, presumably looking for the insect or reptile section.

"Try the table of contents," Jackie said, flipping to the front of her book and the list of topics it covered. "You'll find the page faster than if you just flip through."

That worked for the most part. She managed to make it through the last hours of school without further incident, but at the end of the day when her mother asked them all what they did at school, all Jackie could think of was that she had spent most of lunch recess getting the shade of yellow on her paper snapdragons just right and had been forced to sneak and add the chrysalegg in during science in the afternoon.

Her mother would not have been pleased. Jackie was nervous until Sam accidentally bought her some time by proudly announcing that he had been chosen as student of the week. By the time everyone was done gushing over Sam, Jackie had thought of something better to say.

"I was mostly thinking about my science project," she said. That was true, mostly. It was a science project even if it wasn't an official one for school, and she most certainly had been thinking about it all day. It was almost like it was calling to her. As soon as they got home, she raced to her room to answer.

5
FOR SCIENCE

For the first seven days, nothing happened. Well, something happened. The snapdragon seemed fuller and healthier. The filtered sunlight coming in through her window must have been much more like the sunlight on that mountain in Oregon. Plus, thanks to the air-conditioning, it was much cooler inside. That was probably more like the mountain air in Oregon, too. The delicate yellow petals were more vibrant, and the plant itself had grown at least two inches. With the petals all perky

and bright, they really did look like tiny dragon heads with the jaws open, ready to snap you up.

The chrysalegg, however, looked remarkably the same. At first, her mother had asked her about it every day, thankfully not at the dinner table or anywhere the boys could hear her. She'd poke her head into Jackie's room before bedtime and say,"-Did your plant get any taller?" Then, "Is that chrysalis turning black yet?"

At first, Jackie was saying, "Yes," and "No, not yet" a lot. But after a few weeks, the snapdragon stopped growing, so "Yes," and "No, not yet" turned into a single, "No," which morphed into a tiny shake of the head until, eventually, Jackie's mother stopped asking about the plant and the chrysalegg altogether.

Jackie didn't blame her. The chrysalegg was beginning to bore her, too. She was especially tired of the daily sketch and wished she had never started it because now that she had, it was a pattern, and Jackie hated breaking patterns. It wasn't so much

the sketching part as the daily part that bothered her. Why, oh why hadn't she started sketching it every third day? Or, better yet, every seventh day? There really was no reason to be sketching this thing at all. It never changed. Weren't living things supposed to change? Maybe it wasn't a living thing at all.

She pulled out her drawing things and labeled a new sheet with the date and 'Day 37'. All living things eat, breathe, and grow, right? As far as she could tell, the chrysalegg wasn't doing...

Wait a minute, she thought, pausing to grab her red pencil. Was Jupiter's storm getting smaller? She could have kicked herself. She hadn't measured it before. With all this drawing, how had it never occurred to her to measure the big red spot? She took her ruler out of the drawer, then thought better of it. A wooden ruler couldn't bend to measure around a sphere. (Well, technically it was an ovoid. She had looked it up.) Her mother had a tape measure in her sewing kit, but she didn't like lending them things out of her sewing

kit ever since Jacob and Judah "borrowed" her black thread to make a human-sized spider web. A tape measure wasn't a good idea anyway. She'd probably knock the chrysalegg off the stem trying to wrap the tape measure around it, and if it were alive, that would definitely kill it. How could she measure a spot on something round without touching it? In science class, they had used some little pincer measurement things that looked like crawfish claws. She didn't have any of those, but she did have hairpins.

Jackie fished into one of her french braids and pulled out one of the bobby pins that held it in place. With a little work, she was able to pull the opening of the metal pin enough that it stayed in place instead of snapping back. Then she held it as close to the chrysalegg as she could without touching it, adjusted the opening until it matched the red spot, then measured the opening with her ruler. Two centimeters.

The next night the spot looked much smaller. She adjusted her bobby pin to match the size and mea-

sured it again. It was smaller, but not as much as she expected. The next night the spot looked even smaller, but when she measured it again it was still just a smidge less than two centimeters even though it looked like it had shrunk tremendously.

It wasn't until the fourth night that Jackie realized the spot was looking so much smaller because the chrysalegg was getting bigger! She had been so busy measuring the spot that she didn't notice the chrysalegg had grown to about the size of an ordinary chicken egg. In fact, she wasn't sure she would have realized it if the stalk the chrysalegg was hanging from hadn't been drooping so much. The chrysalegg was really weighing it down. It looked like it might snap at any moment.

Jackie looked around her room for supplies. She pulled four sharpened pencils out of her drawer, dug in a shoebox for that bit of stocking they give you to try on school shoes, and her craft box for some heavy-duty tape. She secured the stocking to the pencils so that it resembled a tent or an awkward hammock, then she drove the pointy

part of the pencils into the dirt and rocks in the flowerpot. The sling was pretty useless right now, but if the chrysalegg got any bigger, it would rest on the sling she had constructed and take some of the strain off the snapdragon stalk.

Stepping back to look at her contraption, Jackie couldn't help feeling a little pleased with herself. Sure, she had seen her father use stockings to support cantaloupes as they grew, but she had adapted it without any help at all. The sharpened pencils particularly were a stroke of genius. Jackie really wanted to share her brilliance with some-one, or at least get to rub it into Jonah's face. What was the point of being brilliant if no one but you knew about it? Plus, the chrysalegg was looking pretty impressive. She was sure that she had nev-er seen anything like it. At lunch recess she had gotten a pass to go to the library to look up moths and butterflies in the area, but nothing seemed quite like this. The librarian—or her mother—probably would have been able to help her do a better search, but no matter how much of her

wanted to share the news, there was always another, bigger part that wanted to keep it for herself. At least for a little while longer. For science, of course.

6
MAGIC

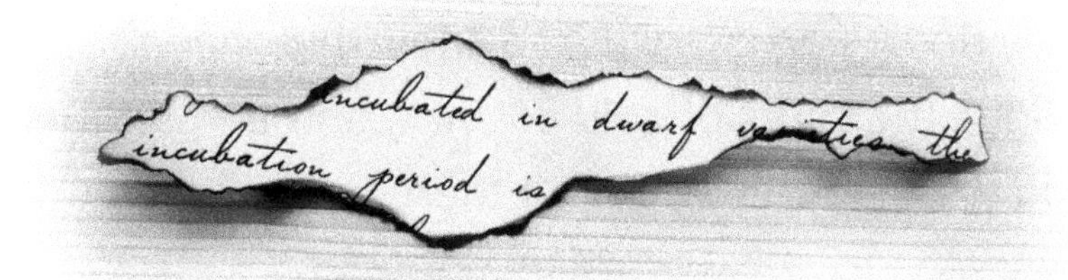

Three days later the chrysalegg was a little bigger than a tennis ball at the bottom and, besides getting bigger, Jackie noticed another change. The red spot, which had shrunk down to less than a quarter of a centimeter, had changed. It was no longer red. Now it was a shiny, metallic gold color.

Jackie was intensely disappointed. Metallic gold would certainly seem magical to anyone who hadn't seen a monarch chrysalis transform. Those flecks of gold seem unreal the first time you see

them. But Jackie had seen monarch transformations happen many times before. So when she saw that the red Jupiter spot had turned metallic gold, she was almost a little upset. Maybe it was just a deformed monarch chrysalis after all. Monarch chrysalises do the exact same thing. Well, they don't start off with red spots, but they do develop little spots of gold so shiny and perfect that you'd swear they were put there by a jeweler.

She had never quite decided what the chrysalegg was, but she had never really thought it was just a butterfly. The gold spot changed her mind. Her mother was probably right. The chrysalegg was just a butterfly—abnormally large, but a butterfly nonetheless. Then a second gold spot appeared. Right before her eyes. As in, one moment there was nothing there, then a ripple faster than a blink, then a new gold spot glittering in the light of her lamp.

Jackie sat perfectly still, willing herself not to blink for fear that she would miss the next spot as it came into being.

She must have fallen asleep because the next thing she knew it was morning, the chrysalegg had a single file line of gold dots stretching from its pointy top to its rounded bottom, and she knew that if she didn't hurry and get ready for school her mother would poke her head in to get her before too long. All she could think about was protecting the chrysalegg. Her mother couldn't see it yet. No one could. She had to keep it hidden.

Jackie got dressed in so much of a hurry that her headband didn't even match her shoes. She grabbed her school bag and started to open her door, but stopped cold. The chrysalegg was now about the size of a Magic 8 Ball and covered in metallic gold dots. If she opened her door and anyone passed by and, let's face it—in a tiny house in the morning someone is always passing by—they couldn't help but see it. If she did something ridiculous like prop up a poster board on her desk that would draw attention, too. Her lamp was kind of tall but wasn't wide enough to cover the snapdragon. That had grown to more than a foot

high and almost a foot across. But the chrysalegg wasn't sitting at the top. Maybe if she pulled her lamp forward a little and angled it so it sort of blocked the view, that would be normal enough to not arouse any suspicion.

It worked. At least Judah didn't say anything when he walked past her open door. She pulled her door mostly closed behind her and tried to make it through breakfast and the drive to school with no mention of the glittery Magic 8 ball growing in her room. All day she prayed that no one had to go back to the house before she did. If one of her brothers got sick at school, her mother or father would leave work to pick them up. And when they picked them up they would bring them home! The thought was so terrifying that she almost faked sick just to make sure she'd have a fighting chance of being the first one to walk in the door. Then she realized that if she were sick her parents would insist on tucking her into bed and there was no way they could miss the chrysalegg if they walked all the way into her room now. Better to hang tight

and hope that Jacob didn't have any tests he was trying to avoid.

By the time the family made it home, Jackie had been worrying for so long that she actually did feel sick. She did some of her homework at the dining room table as usual so as not to arouse suspicion, but when homework time was done and the boys went whooping outside to play, instead of taking her book outside to read on the rocking chair, Jackie went to her room. When she got there, she was almost afraid to push the door open. What if there was an enormous, mutant, killer butterfly flying around her room? Or, worse, what if there was nothing there at all and she had imagined the whole thing?

She hadn't imagined it, of course. When she plucked up the courage to open her door, the chrysalegg was sitting exactly where she had left it, only now the single file line of gold dots wrapped all the way around the egg. A ray of sunlight shone through her window so that each fleck of gold looked like a tiny rainbow. She had won-

dered before, but now there was no doubt. This was definitely magic.

❧

Dinner was a chore. Not only was it next to impossible to sit at a table with other people and NOT tell them about possibly the biggest thing that had ever happened to you, but Jackie was a natural talker. She talked about everything, and at that moment she didn't have anyone she could talk to. Or, rather, she was afraid that if she talked about it, somehow the magic would ooze out like the air in an old tire. She would tell them eventually, of course. If a giant butterfly or something were waiting for her when she got back to her room, there was no way she would be able to keep it to herself. Even if it were possible to keep such a thing secret, and that wasn't likely, Jackie herself would probably explode if she couldn't tell someone how SHE had noticed it, how SHE thought to bring it inside, how SHE had cared for it and protected it, keeping it out of the hands of evildoers until it could fend for itself. And most of all, how SHE had

always believed the chrysalegg was something special when even her mother had not.

She somehow made it through dinner without spontaneously combusting, even though the word magic came up no less than twelve times. So and so did a magic trick. Such and such was almost like magic. Even Sam had asked if they could take a trip to the magic kingdom instead of just saying plain old Disney World.

Jackie's mother kept asking her if she was okay and trying to get her to add in her own details about the day. Jackie did, of course, but it always felt like there was something missing because there WAS something missing.

When she went to scrape her plate in the kitchen, her mother cornered her.

"I think I know what this is about," she said, placing her hand on Jackie's shoulder.

Oh no, Jackie thought, *she knows. She knows about the chrysalegg. And she's being calm about it. Too*

calm. Unnaturally calm. That's not good. Whenever her mother was really calm about something on the surface, it meant that she was trying to control absolute rage underneath. The time she had been the calmest was when Jonah and Judah had filled the cargo area of the van with cereal. And milk.

The worry must have shown on Jackie's face because her mother said, "I knew it would happen someday, I just didn't know it would be this soon. What's his name?"

Jackie shook her head. What was her mother talking about? What's whose name?

"It's perfectly natural, baby," her mother continued, voice smooth. "There's no shame in having a crush on someone. I just never thought it would be so soon..."

Her mother thought she had a crush on someone? She briefly wondered which would be worse, a crush or the fact that she was secretly practic-

ing magic in her room? Neither looked good. She chose option C.

"There's no boy, Mama. It's just," she lowered her voice here for effect, "that I've been drawing a lot lately"--true--"and I haven't wanted to share it with anybody"--also true-- "because John is so good at drawing"--very true--"that I've been afraid that the Js will make fun of me." The last part was less than true, but it wasn't exactly a lie, either. She could imagine the Js finding her drawings and making fun of her for keeping such a detailed log. And she could imagine that if they did that she would feel bad which was pretty much the same as being afraid because afraid was definitely a bad way to feel.

She had been looking down at the floor, mainly to avoid her mother's eyes, but hopefully her mother would interpret that as her feeling embarrassed or something like that. Now she peeked up. Her mother still had a sympathetic look on her face, but that eerie calm was gone.

"Well, whenever you're ready to share them I'd love to see them," Jackie's mom said.

"Of course," Jackie said, relieved. "Soon, Mama."

"Okay. No rush," her mother said, turning to start cleaning the dinner dishes.

Jackie smiled and nodded and turned to go to her room. She had to stop herself from racing so as not to arouse Mama's suspicions again. Even John didn't love drawing enough to race to his room over it. She had to play it at least a little cool.

When she got there the chrysalegg was resting on the sling she had made from pencils and a stocking and tape, but those ordinary things only made it look more extraordinary by contrast. The spots of gold still seemed to sparkle faintly all the way around, even though the afternoon light was no longer streaming through Jackie's window. She closed the door up as much as she dared, took out her drawing things, and labeled the page with the date and 'Day 45.' If the chrysalegg was anything

like a monarch, the pattern of gold spots meant that the butterfly was ready to hatch.

She finished up her drawing and put the drawing things away. She still had homework to do, but the idea of missing the moment when the butterfly emerged so that she could read chapter twelve in her Social Studies book seemed insane. Well, maybe not so insane. They did have a test on Friday. She decided to read through the social studies text and keep an eye on the chrysalegg with her peripheral vision. Peripheral vision was good for catching movement. They had learned that in science a few weeks before.

She finished her social studies. No change. She corrected the two problems she got wrong on her math test and drew an extra credit diagram of an anteater's tongue for science. No change. She put on her pajamas, popping her head through the neck hole as quickly as she could so as not to miss anything. Still no change.

It was getting late. If she wasn't in bed soon, her mother would come in to turn off the light. She had hoped that whatever was going to happen would happen before she had to turn the lights out so that she'd actually get to see it. She had a flashlight, but it wouldn't be safe to turn it on until her mother and father had gone to bed and, depending on the night, that might be right after all the kids were in bed or hours later after hanging out and having what always sounded like a party even though they always claimed it was just the two of them.

Jackie climbed into bed, turned off the light, and waited. Her mother poked her head in and whispered, "Sweet dreams." Jackie pretended to be sleeping. What seemed like hours later, Jackie's dad quietly looked in on her as well. With the door to her parents' room closed, the last little bit of light was gone and Jackie's room was plunged into near-perfect darkness. Jackie kept her eyes closed until she heard the door to her parent's room click softly, then she leaned over the side of

her bed to feel underneath it for where she kept her flashlight. She didn't really need it, though, because magical sparks are even easier to see in the near-perfect dark.

They were tiny at first. Like fairy dust. Or at least how Jackie imagined fairy dust to be. Then there was a tiny pop and a hissing sound, and then flashes of light poured out like sparklers on the 4th of July, but in every color imaginable-red, marigold, emerald, blue, a rainbow of sparkling, fiery light burned brighter and brighter until, suddenly, it stopped.

The shock of the darkness jolted Jackie into reaching for her flashlight again. She found it easily and turned it on, eager to see exactly what had made the fireworks display. The beam from her flashlight landed first on the chrysalegg. Most of it, about two thirds, was hanging as it had been before. A large chunk of it had fallen forward and was dangling precariously from the stocking sling. Jackie moved the beam. Rocks. Leaves. Petals.

And then she saw it. A lizard hanging upside down from a nearby stalk, enormous, scaly wings hanging limply toward the stones below. No, not a lizard. A dragon.

7
JUPITER STORM

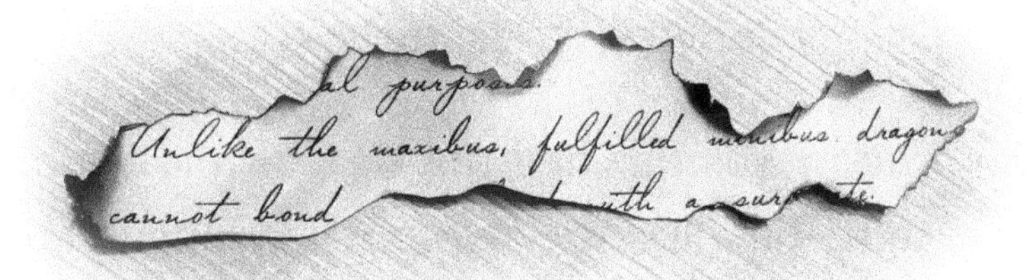

Jackie had never seen a dragon being born. Technically, this was still the case even though it had happened right in front of her, but it wouldn't always be.

She leaned forward, her mouth hanging open a bit. The dragon was amazing. It looked just as she imagined a dragon would. Just as it did in fairy tales, only much, much smaller. The wings were enormous next to the dragon's slender body. Each one was about the size of one of Jackie's hands, but tinted a pale shade of green with

markings that reminded her of the underside of a leaf. Even though they were large, they hung limply like a damp towel on a bathroom rack. On second thought, maybe the wings weren't green at all. Maybe they were translucent. It seemed that the light from the flashlight went right through them, soggy and useless as they were.

The dragon was hanging upside down like a bat from something in the flowerpot. Jackie didn't remember there being a stake or anything solid in there besides the pencils, so she moved the beam from her flashlight up slightly to see where the dragon had attached itself. It was hanging from the very top of one dwarf snapdragon stem, which seemed impossible given how heavy the dragon must have been. But that flower stalk hardly bent at all, where another had been suffering from the weight of the chrysalegg. The more she looked at it, the more she thought that perhaps the snapdragon stood just as straight as it had before, as if there were absolutely nothing on it weighing it down.

She leaned even closer, close enough for the dragon to feel her breath. There was no mistaking what this creature was. Although, as miraculous as it was, she wasn't surprised to see that the dragon was malformed. Or, perhaps dragon wings were always for show. For surely this dragon's limp, lifeless wings would never fly.

Then Jackie remembered something that she knew. It happens that way sometimes. You know something, but you forget you know, and then you remember. When butterflies are born, their wings are also limp and loose because they have been curled up in a tight space. Tight, curled wings would never fly. So when butterflies are born, they hang upside to let their floppy wings hang and dry into a strong, straight shape like laundry on a clothesline. Of course, that's not exactly how that goes, but the principle is the same.

She closed her eyes for a moment, breathing it all in. When she opened them again, she realized how much they had adjusted to the light. She could see the dragon almost perfectly well. It was

mostly green, but she could see that it was many shades of green. Some deeper, some lighter, some almost yellow, some almost black. And here and there, there were hints of purple. It looked familiar somehow, even as it looked strange.

Then it happened. The dragon opened its eyes and their gazes locked. The dragon's eyes were amber. Or gold. It was hard to tell in this light. And the dragon did not look away. Jackie felt as if she knew him. As if she had always known him. And she called him by his name. "Jupiter Storm," she said.

He had emerged from the place on the chrysalis where Jupiter's storm had been. The remnants of chrysalis hanging from the plant and pulling on her stocking sling showed that was true, but even if it hadn't been his name would have been the same. No other one would suit him.

Jupiter Storm and Jackie held each other's gazes for what felt like an eternity. A minute? An hour? She wasn't sure. Then, just as abruptly as it be-

gan, Jupiter Storm closed his eyes, and Jackie saw his wings begin to pulse to life. An intricate web of veins began to fill with blue-green liquid and, as they did, the dragon's wings became firmer and firmer until Jupiter began to slowly flap them. Open. Close. Open. Close. Jackie was nearly hypnotized by the beauty and the smooth, steady motion. Open. Close. Open. Close. Jackie was so in tune with the dragon's movements that it didn't startle her one bit when the dragon took off for its first flight. It seemed only natural. It was what came next. The dragon, her dragon, flapping and gliding around the room with perfect grace.

Jupiter circled Jackie's head once, twice, then Jackie instinctively held her palm up, and her dragon landed there as if he always had. Then Jupiter took a leap toward Jackie's bedroom window. The light from her flashlight had drawn the termites there. They were always terrible at that time of year and would swarm on any poor excuse for a light. When he neared the window, Jupiter pulled up slightly and circled back to Jackie, this time

landing on her shoulder and settling onto one of her thick French braids. He couldn't get outside on his own, but his flight to the window told her everything she needed to know. Her dragon was hungry and, apparently, dragons ate insects.

Jackie had never left the house without permission before, let alone at night. She pushed aside the nagging voice that told her to go wake up her parents and crept as quietly as she could toward the front door.

Their house was tiny which was both good and bad. It was good because it meant that no room was very far from the front door, so she didn't have far to sneak. It was bad because it meant that no room was far from the front door, so the chances that her parents or, worse, one of the Js would hear her sneaking were pretty good, no matter how quickly she went.

She opted for silence and moved as slowly as she could, step by step, carefully placing one bare foot in front of the other on the cool wooden

floor as quietly as possible. She paused between each step, holding her breath and listening to the sound of silence in the house. The refrigerator hum. Judah breathing. Sam sporadically slurping his thumb. Besides her tiptoeing out of the house with a dragon hanging from one of her french braids, everything was perfectly normal.

She made it to the front door and slowly turned the deadbolt, praying it wouldn't click. It didn't. The well-oiled door hinges opened smoothly, and she could feel Jupiter's wings beginning to flap when the moist air rushed to greet them. The spring on the screen door creaked a little, but Jackie held back for a moment to make sure it didn't slam shut. Her dragon, however, could not hold back. Jackie was so caught up in the moment that she didn't think of how foolish it was to bring a flying creature outside with no plan to bring him back in. As soon as the screen door was opened wide enough for him to pass through, Jupiter leaped from Jackie's back and flew straight into the azaleas. By the time Jackie had made it

down the steps, Jupiter was flitting from the azaleas to the verbena to the lantana, flicking his impressively long tongue to snatch up an aphid or two before moving on to the next flower. Jackie almost felt as if she were flying along with him, inhaling the scent of the flowers and growing stronger with every mouthful of food. She sank down onto the steps to watch, mesmerized yet again by the graceful movement of Jupiter's wings.

After a time, Jupiter's almost frantic movements slowed and he spent more time at each stop until he finally came to rest on the azalea bush next to Jackie. He landed with his back claws first, his wings beating back to slow his movement before delicately folding to lie at his side. He felt content after his aphid feast, or, at least Jackie imagined that he did. Content and... powerful. Jupiter pulled his head back and, with an audible croak, let loose a stream of fire that stretched out straight as a rod before splitting into dancing tendrils of flame. Jackie had never seen anything more beautiful. It was so beautiful, in fact, that for a moment she

even forgot to be concerned that there was an open flame pointing directly at her hair. By the time the possibility of her hair catching on fire sank in, Jupiter was already flying again, gobbling up all the aphids in his path. Jackie watched him intently.

The pattern continued like that for some time with Jupiter flying, eating, breathing fire, then flying and eating again. It might have gone on like that until morning if Mrs. Albertine, her neighbor directly across the street, hadn't turned on her porch light.

Mrs. Albertine wasn't married. They just called her that to be polite. She lived with her brother who worked an early shift at the dairy not far from town. Jackie didn't know if Mrs. Albertine's porch light had gone on because her brother was about to leave for work or because she had seen bursts of flame coming from the Johnsons' front yard. Either way it went, Jackie and her dragon needed to get inside before they were found out.

Jupiter was flitting in and out of the lantana, gobbling aphids here and there. He had come to rest on her shoulder several times, but all those times had been of his own accord. Jackie didn't know what would happen if she tried to make him come to her. She couldn't just run over to him and snatch him up. He'd probably be so startled that he would literally fly away, never to be seen again. She couldn't let that happen. He was her dragon, her responsibility. Who knew what would happen if someone found him. Luckily Jackie was fairly skilled at catching wild things, geckos in particular. The trick with wild things was to approach slowly and calmly as if you and your movement were perfectly normal things to be near them like snails or sloths or some other safe piece of the universe. And you had to believe it. Believing it was key.

Out of the corner of her eye, Jackie could see some movement at Mrs. Albertine's window, but since there was nothing to be done about it she decided to press on moving slowly toward the patch of Lantana and squatting almost noiseless-

ly in front of it. Jupiter was within an arm's reach. Her eyes had adjusted to the dark enough to see his tongue flick out, wrap around an aphid, and pull back in one fluid motion. No one likes to be interrupted while they are eating, but this couldn't be helped. She slowly moved her hands out, one flat, one cupped a few inches above it. For geckos she got as close as she could with her hands like that, then, at the last moment, she would use her cupped had to scoop the gecko onto her open one, the cupped hand locking into place like a domed lid. Jupiter's body was about the size of a gecko, but he had wings. Enormous wings. Would she crush them if she clamped down too hard? Would he try to wriggle free? Would he try to burn his way out?

Jupiter did none of those things. While Jackie was crouched in full view of Mrs. Albertine's front porch trying to decide what to do, Jupiter sucked in one last morsel of aphid, stepped onto Jackie's outstretched hand, circled once, and then settled

into a cat-like sleeping ball on Jackie's palm with his wings all tucked in around him.

The first time a dragon curls up to sleep on your palm can only be described as adorable, but Jackie didn't have time to savor it. She could hear Mrs. Albertine beginning to unlock her door. Luckily, Mrs. Albertine was a bit paranoid about intruders and had no less than seven locks and latches, which gave Jackie plenty of time to scurry inside with no one the wiser.

8
DRAGON BED

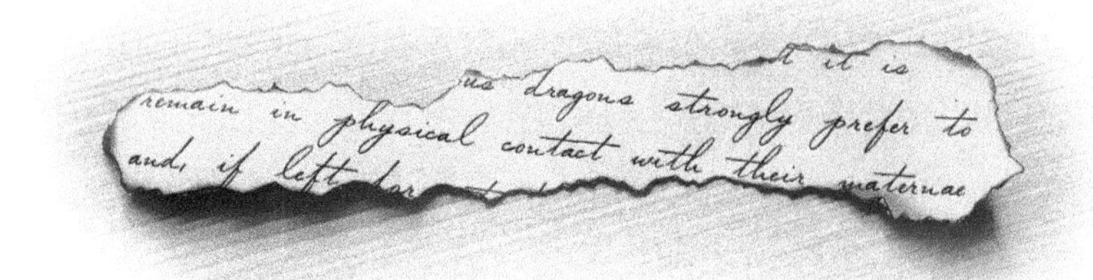

Bringing a fire-breathing dragon, even a relatively small one, into your room requires caution because, well, fire.

It was a little past two o'clock in the morning, and as the adrenaline rush began to wear off, Jackie found herself thinking of sleep more and more seriously which, in turn, brought her back around to the knowledge that she had a fire-breathing dragon in her room. Jupiter's flames were very small, but it didn't take much to catch things on fire. Even

a tiny flame would do the job. She looked around her room. Books, wooden desk, bed sheets... Why had it never occurred to her that practically everything she owned was flammable? *What did people do back before there was electricity?* she thought. *They had to use candles for light at night, right?* But that wasn't very helpful because the answer was put out their candles or accidentally set the house on fire.

Jupiter was curled up on her shoulder with his tail lacing through one of her french braids. He wasn't sleeping, but he did seem tired. Even a dragon would need to sleep sometime, though, wouldn't it? Would it? Were dragons nocturnal, diurnal, or crepuscular like cats? She had no way of knowing for sure. Not yet. It was night time, and Jupiter had been very active, but maybe that was just because he was hungry. Being born takes a lot of energy, so it wasn't surprising that he had spent so much time eating. Even human babies nursed a bunch right after they were born.

Jupiter adjusted his wings and snuggled in a bit more. His scales were smooth and warmed quickly against her neck. Maybe they could just sleep together. Lots of mamas slept with their babies. Sam had slept in her parents' bed for years. *What was the big deal?* she thought, settling onto her bed. Jupiter seemed comfortable. She was comfortable. It was only a few hours until morning. What could go wrong?

The problem with being a thinker is that you'll answer your own questions, even when you're drifting off to sleep. *Set your hair on fire*, she thought, bolting upright on her bed, the sleep-fog lifting immediately. Jackie wasn't vain. Not really. Sure, she liked fancy shoes. But Jackie didn't wear fancy shoes because they made her beautiful. She wore them because THEY were beautiful. And who doesn't like to be surrounded by beautiful things? And Jackie did like the way she looked—chestnut skin, dark eyes, and a light smattering of freckles if you looked closely enough—but she didn't sit around staring at herself in the mirror, thinking

about how lovely she was. And when someone paid her a compliment about her smile she just said thank you without feeling even a tiny blush of pride. Her hair, on the other hand, was another story. It was long and thick and filled with so many bumps and twists and turns that it was like a roller coaster ride or a stormy sea. When people commented on how long and thick it was or, most especially, the beauty of its texture, Jackie felt a rush of pride, even if the comment was more a fact than a compliment. She was careful to tie her hair down with a scarf every night and decorate it with barrettes or a headband every morning. So, suffice it to say that the thought of waking up with her hair on fire knocked her back into action.

She scanned the room. The snapdragon pot, the toy shelf, and her bookshelf were all quickly eliminated, not so much because they were flammable as because they were open. Jupiter seemed so comfortable where he was that he might just fly back there after she fell asleep if he were on one of those open places. The closet was an option. He

couldn't fly out of there if she closed the door, but if he breathed fire on her clothes with the door shut she probably wouldn't realize that there was a fire at all until it had gotten out of hand. Better not risk it. Then she remembered the terrarium. It was off to the side of her desk in a hidden corner of her room so her mother wouldn't constantly be reminded of the gecko debacle. The sides were made of glass. The top and bottom were made of metal. There was enough room in there for Jupiter to turn around and spread his wings and maybe even flap around a bit. It was perfect!

Jackie set about preparing the terrarium for Jupiter to sleep in. She moved some rocks and soil from the snapdragon pot to line the bottom. Most of the snapdragon was too tall to fit inside the terrarium, so she tried to unearth a few young stalks without damaging their roots and replanted them propped up in one corner. Then, in a fit of inspiration, she dumped out the pen and pencil can from her desk and put it in the terrarium, too. It was just an empty can of corn she had painted in

a craft project, but it really put the finishing touch on the terrarium. Now instead of feeling like she was putting Jupiter in a cage, she felt like she was putting him to bed.

Jupiter was a little less certain. He let her lift him from her shoulder with no problem, but he either wouldn't or couldn't loosen his tale from inside of her braid. Eventually, she had to unbraid it some to pull his tail free. Once he was inside his new bed, he climbed into the can as if it were a cave and settled down to sleep. Jackie placed the lid on the terrarium and put a few of the larger rocks on top to keep it in place. Jupiter might still be able to knock them free if he tried hard enough, but that was the best she could do.

Jackie fell asleep quickly, but she had never slept more fitfully, not even on Christmas Eve. And saying that she fell asleep wasn't quite right, either, since she never felt herself drifting off. She only felt the part where she woke up, her heart racing with panic so that she scrambled over to check on him one more time. Then one more time. She

got up five times before the sky even showed a hint of morning. Jupiter stirred a little every time she checked on him, but that might have been because her jumping up every five seconds was disturbing him. Every time she would pop straight up still clutching the flashlight in her right hand. She clicked on the beam, threw back the covers, and went to kneel in front of the terrarium, the light from the flashlight shining directly on him.

There was no denying the relief she felt every time she moved her flashlight to the corner beside her desk and saw Jupiter there, his dappled green body at attention, his eyes fixed directly on her. She would kneel in front of him and just stare.

Jupiter was there. He was real. He was still with her.

The thought made her heart flutter and, for once, she didn't try to think of what the ending would be. She couldn't. There was too much to see right in front of her. By the time she had calmed down enough to climb back into bed and get settled un-

der the covers, Jupiter was already sleeping. At least that's the way it looked by the glow of the flashlight. From all the way across the room, it was hard to be sure.

Everything's okay, she thought. *You're fine.* But since she didn't dare start talking aloud, she really was just talking to herself.

Jackie woke several hours later, her loosened braid sticking to her neck, bright sunlight streaming through her window. She had no idea what time it was, but it was definitely late. Not that they had anywhere in particular to be. There was no school on Saturday, and her mother and father both agreed that they should all have at least one day that wasn't filled up with planned activities. Cooking dinner, going to church and eating dinner always took up the whole of a Sunday, so that left Saturday as their day to be free.

On Saturdays, the Js got up at first light. Jacob, Jonah, and Judah would be off as soon as possible to ride bikes, play football in the street, or slide down the levee on flattened cardboard boxes. John might have slept in a bit, but once Sam was up, there was no way he'd let John sleep. Who would be the audience for his animal cards? He had about 300 of them, and he loved to use them to quiz people on animal facts. For Sam, it was a game that never got boring. He used to quiz everyone, but mama got tired of picking up trails of animal cards all over the house, and she eventually restricted Sam's animal cards to his room. The other boys escaped the quizzing now by avoiding Sam's room, but since Sam and John shared a room, John wasn't so lucky. John was mostly a good sport about it, but Jackie made sure to go in and relieve him sometimes, especially on Saturday mornings.

The floor of their room was littered with animal cards, but Sam and John were nowhere around when she passed their room to use the bath-

room. She splashed water on her face and did her best to re-braid the plait she had loosened. Luckily it hadn't unbraided all the way to her scalp. She could do plaits, but she didn't know how to do scalp braids. When she was done her repaired braid had a slight Pippi Longstocking bend to it which wasn't ideal, but she had more important things to do. Jupiter Storm was waiting for her.

Before she had left for the bathroom, Jupiter looked hopeful, almost eager to see her. He had flapped his wings and stretched his neck and given every possible indication that he was ready to get out of his "bed." She couldn't just let him fly around in her room, though. That was too risky. So she had left him with quiet assurances that she would be back as soon as possible. When she returned, he beat his wings so insistently that she could practically hear him speak.

Fly! he was saying. We must fly.

"I know," Jackie said aloud. "I know. You don't want to be cooped up in there. Just give me a minute

to figure something out." She wasn't sure what she was figuring out. There was no way she could bring him outside. Outside was filled with eyes—the neighbors', her brothers'. There was even a hawk that flew around sometimes. It seemed just as impossible to bring Jupiter outside, though, as it did to leave him trapped in a terrarium all day. Inside he was safe. Maybe she could just scrape off some aphids and bring them inside. Jupiter liked aphids. He had practically eaten his weight in aphids the night before. How much did he weigh, exactly? He obviously didn't weigh much. Whenever he landed on a flower, he didn't disturb it much more than a butterfly would. But aphids were even smaller and lighter than butterflies. How many aphids would she need to bring inside for him? How would she know when he was full? Would he even eat them if they weren't on flowers? She had read about how pet snakes needed to be trained to eat frozen mice since their natural instinct was to hunt then eat. Maybe Jupiter was like that. Besides, if her mother caught her bringing a container filled with aphids into the house,

she couldn't even imagine the levels of creepy Zen she would be subjected to. It would probably be better to get caught with the dragon.

Well, if feeding Jupiter inside was out, the only other option was to smuggle him outside.

9
THE JUNGLE

production and, as a result, bonding is an essential element in flame production. They

Saturday mornings were the closest her parents ever got to being lazy. Even though there were chores to do—grass to be cut, windows to be washed, groceries to be made—her parents had made a solemn yet silent pact to do none of it before 10:00 a.m. After the breakfast table was cleared Jackie's mother would get whatever she was reading and Jackie's father would get whatever he was reading, and they would both read together on the sofa in the living room. They didn't talk. They didn't

read aloud to each other. They just sat there, Jackie's mother using her father's lap as a pillow, Jackie's father absently stroking her mother's hair. Sometimes her parents were so absorbed in their books that they didn't even notice the children passing unless someone said, "Blood."

Jackie's parents weren't snuggled up on the sofa, though. Her father was making a grocery list, and her mother was under the sink, possibly fixing the dripping faucet.

"Never seen you sleep so late," her father said. "Do we need eggs, Vi?"

"I don't know. Would you like to come finish the sink while I check for you?"

Her father said something unintelligible as he moved from the counter to the fridge to check the egg carton.

"Are you feeling okay, baby?" Her mother asked, poking her head out from under the sink. "I went

in to check on you earlier. You didn't have a fever, so I figured you were just tired."

Jackie nodded frantically. Her mother had what? Jupiter was right there! Had she seen? But before full-scale panic took hold, Jackie took a deep breath and quietly calmed herself. The terrarium was tucked in the same little corner it had been in for ages. If Jupiter wasn't making noise, there was nothing that would draw her mother's attention about it. Besides, if her mother had found Jupiter, there's no way she would be finding out about it after peacefully sleeping in.

"I'm just tired, Mama. I don't know why."

Jackie's parents exchanged a look.

"Well," her mother began carefully, "you're getting older and as your body starts to change it's not unusual for you to need more sleep than you did before."

"Mom!" Jackie said. Her parents had been doing the puberty talk with her in the most painful way

possible—tiny snippets stretched out over an eternity. "I'm not going through puberty. I've just been doing a lot of extra work for school. Miss Soraparu is so impressed that she said I might get the Young Scientist award this year." Her teacher, Miss Soraparu, had said that. Jackie didn't need to mention that she had said it several months before because that would just cloud the issue.

"Well, you missed breakfast. Jacob cleaned out the grits pot, but you could fix yourself something to hold you over until lunch."

"Can I go on an expedition?" Jackie asked. An expedition. She hadn't even thought about it consciously, so when the words came out of her mouth so smoothly she impressed herself with her own genius. Whichever part of her brain had stumbled upon the perfect solution without her knowledge deserved a raise. An expedition was a perfect plan.

The front of the Johnsons' house was perfectly neat. Swept porch. Fluffed pillows. Beautifully

tended flower beds. Jackie and her mother were in charge of the front of the house. Her father was in charge of the back, and it was a jungle. Not literally, of course. But nearly. Jackie's father was fond of "gifts from the birds" that her mother called "weeds."

Every time a wild thing grew in an odd place in the backyard, Jackie's father would say, "I wonder what the birds have brought us," and then he'd wait to see what it would become. The milkweed had been a gift from the birds. So had the night blooming jasmine and bananas and some kind of plant that turned from scrawny weed to sapling in less than a week. Her mother couldn't take the chaos, but her father loved it, and so did she. It was their own private kingdom, complete with fire pit and a partially built brick oven that looked like Mayan ruins hidden in thick foliage. You could get lost back there even though the fence was no more than fifty feet away. Periodically Jackie's father would go beat it back, but it filled back in al-

most as soon as he had, like digging a hole in dry sand.

An expedition into the jungle was not an everyday thing, even for archaeologists, but ever since Jackie was Sam's age she had enjoyed packing a picnic and spending the day (and, once, a whole night) out there. Even when they were little, Jacob had never joined her. He liked playing outside, but he hated bugs so he wouldn't go where the foliage was thick. John had joined her a time or two, but it wasn't his cup of tea, and she had threatened Jonah and Judah so thoroughly about ripping off flowers and leaves for no good reason that they both pretty much steered clear. It was perfect. She just needed to wrap Jupiter up in the picnic blanket, stuff that in the basket, then run outside as quickly as she could before he made noise or completely set the basket on fire. A small fire she could just stomp out when she got outside.

She was so busy plotting in her mind that she almost missed when her mother said, "Jacquelyn Marie, it is unladylike to urinate in the yard."

She wished she had missed it. Why was her mother bringing this up again for the hundredth time? Sure, she had urinated in the yard probably dozens of times, but she had only been caught the once. Why was her mother making such a big deal about something that only happened once?

Seeing that her father was not about to come to her rescue, Jackie swallowed her pride and said, "Yes, Ma'am."

"Ok. But make sure you bring all my containers back inside and shake off whatever blanket you use before you put it in the washing machine. The last time I kept finding twigs in the laundry for days afterward."

"Yes, Ma'am," Jackie repeated, getting the step ladder so she could pull the picnic basket off the high shelf.

"And make sure you clean out the containers and put the basket back without anyone having to remind you."

"Yes, Ma'am."

"And when you wash the blankets, make sure you put them straight into the dryer so they don't mildew."

"Yes, Ma'am."

"And..." Jackie stood poised for more instruction, but her mother must not have been able to think of anything else because she ducked her head back under the sink and finished with, "when you come in, you're in, but don't make me have to send a search party to get you for dinner."

Her father gave her a quick smile, but then got his car keys from the hook in the kitchen and headed out the front door with the grocery list.

Smuggling a dragon in a blanket went smoother than Jackie expected. She stepped out onto the back steps with the picnic basket hanging from the crook of her arm looking for all the world like

Dorothy or Alice, right down to her twirly dress and fancy little shoes. Her lavender shoes looked beautiful running through the tall grass, and there was nothing quite like the feeling of a fluffy skirt flying behind you as you pick up enough speed to run. Some people think dresses are not good clothes for playing, but Jackie was wise enough to know that the only real trick to wearing a dress on an expedition was to not care if it got ruined.

She raced past the chairs and the fire pit, ducking under vines and jumping over stray bricks and useless paving stones until she got to a little clearing near the fence at the back of the yard. It was only a clearing because she made it one, and every time she went outside she had to clear it again. But it was worth the effort. There was a kumquat tree her father had planted and forgotten years before and a baby loquat tree that had sprung up on its own. She was far enough from the house that no one could see her from the back windows, and the chainlink fence was so covered with morning glories that it was as private as a wooden one.

Normally she would have started by clearing all the fallen kumquats and loquats and new weeds from the area, but today there were more important things. She had to let Jupiter out so he could breathe.

She opened the basket carefully, peeking at the contents inside as if she wasn't sure what she would find. Jupiter was there among the containers of fruit and bottles of water, curled up in a sheet as though it were a cave. Their eyes met, and Jackie's heart leaped. It was all so strange, but the strangest part was how normal it felt.

Jupiter stretched his wings. They unfolded like an umbrella, knocking the sheet away as they emerged. In the dappled sunlight, they were even more beautiful than she remembered. And strong. Those wings were meant to fly.

Jupiter beat his wings and flew up to land on her shoulder for a moment before flying toward a line of red ants. She watched him for a while. Here he was free. He could fly around without being seen.

Every beat of his wings was like a heartbeat. Jackie could almost feel it.

After a while Jupiter came to rest again on her shoulder, nestling into her hair like a barrette. She wondered if he looked like a barrette. Maybe she could bring him places and just pretend that he was some kind of elaborate hair ornament. Probably not a good idea, she laughed to herself. Especially not when her barrette suddenly flew away and started eating beetles or something. Did he eat beetles? she wondered as she started clearing the area where she would lay her blanket. *Probably*, she thought, tossing the taller weeds onto a little pile. The smaller ones would just get smushed by the weight of the blanket, so she didn't bother with them.

Before long, her base camp was set up just the way she liked it. A double layer of blanket weighted down by the picnic basket on one corner, her shoes with the socks tucked neatly inside on another. She left the food in the basket until she wanted to eat it, but she kept her water bottle

near her at all times. That and a marble notebook that she used as her expedition journal. When she was younger, she filled it with all of her adventures, including the time she had defeated the crocodile from Peter Pan (whom she always called Monsieur Cocodrille even though she knew that wasn't his name) and Jean Lafitte on that very spot. She flipped past the monkey invasion and the journey to the Mayan temple where she had narrowly escaped with her life. Then there were the unicorns she tamed and all the pages where a stuffed animal or two from her school had been allowed to venture afield until she finally came to a clean sheet near the end.

John would do a far better job with the sketch. If John did it, it would look like Jupiter was about fly right off the page. Hers looked more like a diagram. Jupiter watched from her shoulder, and Jackie found herself asking his opinion.

"What do you think?" Silence from Jupiter. "You're right. Your wings are much wider than I have them. You'd never be able to fly if your wings were that

small." Jupiter flapped his wings and the breeze they made tickled the side of her neck.

"What about your tail?" she said. Jupiter made a noise as if in answer. "I know it's not right. But I can only draw what I see, and I can't really see it when it's stuck in my hair like that." Jupiter did not pull his tail free so that she could take a closer look, but she got a good look not too long after when he dove from her shoulder to gobble a gnat hovering just above the grass. His wings barely cast a shadow, and his tail flew out behind him like a leaf on a vine. Jackie sketched it quickly and then sat watching him for a long time. He only breathed fire twice. The first time a quick spark right after he had eaten some ants. The second time, though, he emitted a narrow stream of blue and white almost half as long as he was. That caught Jackie's attention. She sat up straight and put herself in easy reach of her shoes so that she could use them to stomp out the flames if need be. A fire like that could really do some damage. But Jupiter seemed content after his rather im-

pressive show, and just flitted back and forth, eating and resting in a rhythmic pattern that almost put Jackie to sleep. The food. The wings. The air. She didn't need anything more. She drifted off to sleep on her blanket, a warm spring breeze caressing her neck. Before long Jupiter settled into his favorite spot, dozing there as if he had always belonged there.

They spent most of the day like that. Jackie woke occasionally for a sip of water, but Jupiter barely stirred. Once she thought she heard footsteps, but realized that it was probably just one of the Js getting a ball that had strayed into the side yard. Nothing to worry about. With the oven and the vines blocking the view, they would have to get really close to be able to see anything, and if that happened, she would have plenty of warning to tuck Jupiter in the picnic basket and hope for the best.

She woke in the late afternoon feeling ravenous. It must have been close to dinner time, but despite her hunger, she wasn't ready to go inside yet. Her

mother had a strict no in and out rule, so once you were in, you were in, even if the whole world was still outside having fun. Jackie wasn't ready, and Jupiter didn't seem ready, either. Their nap had rejuvenated him, and he was gliding back and forth between higher and higher branches in the kumquat tree until he made for a magnolia tree in her neighbor's yard.

It made her nervous for him to be so high up, so far away. She wanted him to come back to her, but she didn't know how to call him. How do you call a dragon? Can you call a dragon? He had come to land on her hand and shoulder lots of times before, but that was when he wanted to, not because she called him. Maybe if she put something tasty in her hand, she could train him to land there on command.

Jackie had never had a dog, but it seemed as though people who had dogs trained them to sit and stay and roll over with stern looks and the promise of a treat. Having perfected her stern look long ago, Jackie searched around for a drag-

on treat. Her eyes landed on the red ant hill Jupiter had been feasting on earlier, but since no one is that foolish, she kept scanning. There was a stray brick a couple of steps away from the blanket. It was either from the oven or from one of her father's abandoned attempts at a flower bed. Either way, it looked like the brick had been sitting there for a while, which made it a perfect hiding spot for roly-polies.

Sure enough, the brick was covering two roly-polies and a worm. The worm made a dash for it, but the roly-polies did what roly-polies do. They rolled up into little balls. Jackie picked one of them up gingerly with practiced fingers and placed it in the middle of her palm. She turned to face Jupiter, holding up her outstretched hand so that he could see the roly-poly there.

"Jupiter, come," she said. Jupiter stretched his wings wide and dove, gliding toward her effortlessly before pulling up slightly to land on her palm. The little ball of roly-poly rolled around when Jupiter landed, but it didn't uncurl. Jupiter

didn't seem to notice it. He was looking at Jackie and Jackie was looking at him.

"Good job, Jupiter. Good job," she whispered. This was the part where she fed him the dragon treat as a reward for coming. But he didn't eat the treat. Even when the roly-poly foolishly decided that it was safe to crawl away, Jupiter didn't pay it any mind.

"You don't like roly-polies?" Jackie said, using one finger to stroke the back of Jupiter's head. He seemed to like it. "Or are you just not hungry?"

"He doesn't eat that," Sam said.

Jackie whipped around. Her mind flooded with panic. She couldn't breathe. She could barely see. Jupiter flapped his wings restlessly. This was the end.

"See," he said, holding up an animal card for Jackie to look at. "They eat ants and termites. That's a roly-poly."

Jackie leaned forward to look at what Sam was holding. Her whole body was trembling. She could barely make out the words on the card. Thankfully "Draco Lizard" was printed in large, clear letters right across the top.

She had seen this card before. She remembered thinking that the draco looked cool, but now she couldn't see why she thought that. The lizard on the card looked pretty ordinary. It certainly looked nothing like Jupiter Storm. Well, they did bear a tiny resemblance in the body, but those pathetic flaps of skin sticking out from the draco's sides were nothing like Jupiter's wings. But still...

"Do you want to pet him?" She knelt down next to Sam and held Jupiter out toward him, her hand steady.

Sam nodded, cautiously reaching out to touch Jackie's "pet draco" with one finger. "Where did you get it?"

"From school. Wait. Not like that," she said, pausing to catch Sam's hand. He was stroking Jupiter against the direction of his scales. That didn't feel good to him. "Like this. Softly and down. See? He likes it." Jupiter folded his wings and wrapped himself up like a cat, letting Sam continue to stroke his head and back. "Mr. Fowler didn't want him anymore, so he gave him to me as a prize for being the best at science."

"Cool!" Sam said. "What's his name?"

"Jupiter Storm."

"That's a cool name."

"It is, right? Mr. Fowler called him Jumper, but that wasn't a cool enough name for him. I had to think of something better."

"Where does he sleep?"

"In the terrarium in my room."

"I didn't know you had a terrarium in your room."

"Yeah. It's been there since you were little. Do you want to see it?"

Sam nodded eagerly. Jackie hardly ever let any of the boys into her room, so it's possible that Sam was as excited to go in there as he was to see where the 'draco' slept.

"Okay, but on one condition." Jackie continued, "It has to be our secret." Sam didn't say anything, so Jackie kept talking. "Mama doesn't know. If she finds out, she'll make me give Jupiter back to Mr. Fowler. You know how Mama feels about animals in the house. Do you want me to have to give him back, Sam?"

Sam looked down at Jupiter. He was quiet, and Jackie thought maybe she had better give him room to think. Finally, he looked up and said. "I want us to keep him."

"Okay. So, will you promise not to tell anyone?"

Sam nodded again, holding out his pinky finger. "I promise." He looked so solemn, like a little knight swearing an oath of fealty.

Jackie linked her pinky into his. "Good! It's getting late. We should put Jupiter to bed and call the boys inside before Mama starts looking for us. Think you can help me?"

Sam nodded.

"Good. Let's get to work. You put the stuff back in the basket, and I'll shake out the blankets."

"Can I hold Jupiter?"

Jackie was sitting to put on her socks and shoes with Jupiter still balanced on one hand. "Not right now. Maybe later."

"Do you promise?"

"Yeah. I promise."

10
SAM

Sam was cooler than Jackie had given him credit for. She actually started to like having him in her room all the time. He never asked if he could. He just came and climbed in her bed before light one morning, and she didn't tell him to stop.

It was kind of nice. He was like a warm little teddy bear curled up next to her. She liked threading her fingers through the tight coils of his hair and feeling it spring back into place. Then at first light,

they would both check on Jupiter Storm. He was always awake when they looked.

It was actually Sam who pointed out that if Jupiter ate insects, then Jupiter should go outside when there were the most insects, in the evening and early morning. That made sense. And it also made sense that those were the times when Jupiter was the most active.

Jackie let it be known that it was getting too hot to water the garden right before school as she usually did. She'd get sweaty and feel like she needed to take another bath right before school started. Nobody took much notice. It was getting hot, after all. And not even Jacob wanted to start the school day off sweaty and gross. So Jackie and Sam started taking Jupiter out first thing in the morning. Jackie would water the garden, Jupiter would eat his fill of aphids and ants and whatever he could find, and Sam was the lookout.

Jackie didn't really trust Sam to be the lookout, but she had tried letting him water the flowers while

she watched for people coming or going, and that was a disaster. Some flowers he drowned. Others got no water at all. Then there was the fact that he either couldn't or wouldn't use the sprayer without wetting himself from head to toe. A bunch of wet clothes mildewing up the dirty clothes hamper was a surefire way to draw their mother's attention, so Jackie let Sam stand watch. He took it surprisingly seriously, which was pretty adorable in and of itself. That turned out to be a good decision. With such a cute little guard on duty, there was much less chance that any passersby would notice the dragon flying around their front yard because they would be too distracted by Sam's adorableness.

It especially worked well in the mornings, because in the morning everybody is thinking about where they need to be instead of paying attention to where they are. The evenings were trickier, though. Not just because people were paying more attention, but because the time when Jackie and Sam needed to be inside for dinner and

washing up was exactly when Jupiter yearned to be outside the most.

At first, Jackie and Sam had tried bringing some critters inside in a lunch container that Jackie claimed to have lost at school. Their mother kept a strict count on lunch containers, but Jackie figured that since she hadn't lost one yet and Jupiter was her dragon, that saying it was lost was the best way to explain why it was missing, and it was up to her to stand in the line of fire.

Since it was only her first "lost" container, their mother let Jackie off with a warning. The warning was wasted, though, because the container full of bugs didn't work. As soon as they took the top off Jupiter's bed, he would fly in circles past Jackie's window. She could get him to come back to her, but she couldn't get him to eat the bugs from the container. Not really. Even though she knew he was hungry.

After a few days of that, Jackie felt certain Jupiter would starve, but she couldn't think of a good

enough excuse to leave the house after dinner even once, let alone every day. The only thing for it was to let Jupiter go out in the evening alone.

The first time they did, it was right after dinner. Sam wanted to join her, but he seemed to take the hint when she gently reminded him that he needed to take a bath. That was the time when Jackie would normally finish up her homework or tinker around quietly in her room waiting for her turn in the bathroom. They went in reverse age order, so she was second to last.

Once she could hear her mother and Sam in the bathroom, she opened one of the windows in her room wide and closed up her room door as much as she could before bringing Jupiter over to the window.

Warm, moist air rushed in. Jupiter seemed hesitant to leave her at first, but the sight of a mosquito hawk on the edge of the porch sent him flying. He swooped down, scooped up the mosquito

hawk with his mouth and flew back to Jackie in a single arc.

It didn't take much encouragement for him to fly out a second time, and a third. Even though there was still some daylight left, the street light had turned on, and the termites were beginning to swarm near it.

Jupiter leaped out, gliding at first then flapping to get higher and higher. From Jackie's window, he looked something like a bat circling among the termites, gobbling them up in midair. He felt so close. The lamp post was at least twenty feet away, and the light at the top was just as high. Jupiter had never ranged so far from her, and yet she felt that at any moment she could reach out and touch him, the termites so close that she had to resist the urge to swat them out of her own face.

The sound of Jonah and Judah arguing in the hallway about whose turn it was to clean the tub startled her out of her daydream. She put her hand

out and said, "Jupiter. Come." Her voice was quiet. In her room with a house full of people, she could not be as clear and commanding as she usually was, but Jupiter seemed to hear her and respond all the same. He flew to her and landed in her hand. Instead of letting him climb up to her shoulder as she usually did, she walked him over to his bed and placed him inside. Then she counted backward from ten in her mind before taking him out again and bringing him back to the window. That time he flew straight to the streetlight, hovering, turning, swirling. The rush of the air was divine, but Jackie did not let herself get caught up. She stuck her hand out of the window and called him, even more quietly this time. He came immediately and allowed her to put him to bed. She counted backward from twenty that time and repeated the pattern until Jupiter flew back on his own and stayed in bed for two full minutes of his own accord. By that time, they were both exhausted, but Jackie felt quite pleased with herself. Her dragon was smart. She doubted she could have trained a dog so quickly.

Jackie reached in to stroke Jupiter on his favorite spot, the back of his head where his head joined his body. Sam walked in just as she was about to put the top on the terrarium.

"Can I pet him?" Sam asked.

Even though it had been weeks, Jackie was still hesitant about letting Sam touch Jupiter. Jupiter was hers. At least he was her responsibility. And he was one of a kind. Sam would never hurt Jupiter on purpose, but accident or on purpose, if her dragon got hurt that would be disastrous. What could she do? Take him to the vet?

It was hard to tell Sam no all the time, though. She had run out of legitimate excuses to stop him from petting Jupiter the week before. Jupiter didn't bite. He didn't rear up or back away when Sam approached. And Sam had never seen Jupiter breathe fire. In fact, the last time Jupiter had breathed fire at all was on their first expedition in The Jungle, and thankfully Sam had missed that part.

Jackie put on a happy face and grudgingly moved aside for Sam to pet Jupiter. She needed Sam on her side. If sharing Jupiter was the price she paid to stop Sam from blabbing, so be it.

"That's enough," she said after a few seconds. Sam looked up at her quizzically. "Mama will come looking for you in a minute if you're not in bed." Sam's head dropped, but he nodded and let Jackie put the lid in place without protest.

Sam's little sad face was the kind of adorable that made everyone feel guilty, even if they hadn't done anything. Jackie squatted down to look him right in the eye. Jackie was small for her age, so she didn't have to squat much.

"Do you want me to carry you to room?"

Sam perked up. He loved piggyback rides, and he nodded eagerly as he ran around to scramble up on Jackie's back.

"Can I hold him tomorrow?"

"Maybe tomorrow," she said for what felt like the millionth time.

That was their pattern for a while. Jackie's mother thought it was sweet that Jackie was taking such an interest in Sam, and besides her father mentioning the A/C "not cooling like it used to," Jupiter's evening flights went unnoticed, partially because Jackie took to letting Jupiter hunt while her family was eating dinner. Sometimes he went as far as the Magnolia tree behind The Jungle, but usually, he kept to the front yard. Jackie liked watching him searching the flower beds for aphids when she returned to her room after dinner. He did a better job with that than she ever could have and the flowers were happy for his attention. It seemed they could go on like that forever. If only they could have.

11
THE REPORT

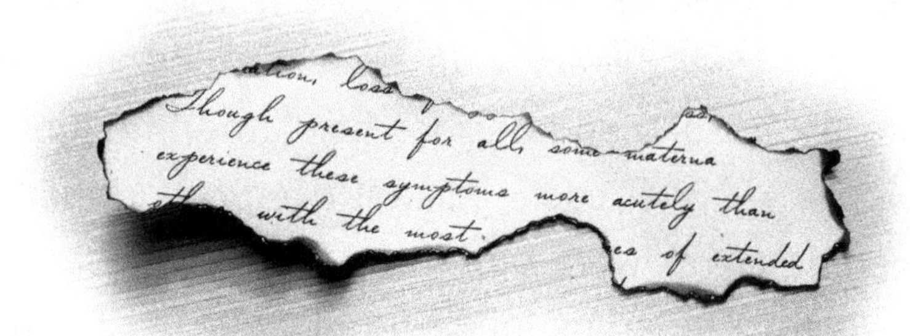

It was Monday. Jackie scooted her chair in and tried to shake the nagging feeling that she had forgotten something. Her mother had rebraided her hair that morning. She was wearing a new headband that matched her favorite pencil case, but it wasn't as exciting as it should have been. For some reason, all she could think about was Jupiter. He was in the terrarium. She didn't call it his bed anymore because he had made it plain that

he would rather sleep in her bed, nestled in her hair or curled up as close to her as he could get.

She didn't like having to leave him cooped up all day, but what else could she do? She couldn't just let him fly around. He hadn't breathed fire in weeks, but she still couldn't leave him loose in the house. Maybe if she knew he would stay in her room. But not being able to shut her room door all the way meant that Jupiter could slip through the cracked door and fly anywhere in the house. That had disaster written all over it. And if she let him fly around outside unguarded, the best-case scenario was that he would follow her to school, and she knew how that would go. Children always see things grown-ups miss.

Jackie had unpacked her backpack and stacked her things neatly in her desk, squaring up the corners of the books and folders out of habit. Her friend Ashley had just arrived and was unpacking next to her. She smiled back at Ashley when Ashley said hi, but that was about it. Ashley took the hint and after unpacking went over to another group

of desks and started chatting with a girl named Miriam instead. They were looking at something in Miriam's paper doll folder and laughing quietly.

Ordinarily, Jackie would have joined them, but her mind was on Jupiter. She played the morning over and over in her mind, trying to figure out what she had forgotten. She and Sam had taken Jupiter out that morning as usual. He had seemed less interested in food than flying. By then he had pretty much wiped out the aphid population in the front garden, so while Sam stood guard over Jackie watering the flowers, Jupiter flew in higher and higher spirals over the top of the house and into the backyard. Jupiter flying out of sight still made her nervous, but she was less concerned about that now than she had been. She knew that if she called him, he would come back to her almost immediately, so he must not have gone too far.

When she was done watering the flowers, she would stand on the front porch right next to her open window and call him quietly. When Jupiter landed on her hand, she would pass him through

the window and close it from the outside. Sam was waiting in her room to make sure Jupiter didn't fly out before Jackie made it inside. That gave Sam some alone time with Jupiter which Sam loved. Jackie wasn't thrilled about it, but it was necessary. She couldn't keep finding excuses for bringing the picnic basket out on the front porch in the morning, and she couldn't risk being seen with Jupiter walking back into the house. They went out early, but you never knew.

Had she maybe forgotten to put the rocks on top of the terrarium? She thought she had, but she wasn't certain. Maybe she was remembering it from another day.

"Good morning, Scientists." Miss Soraparu never called them "Class" or "Children." She always said something like "readers," "writers," or "mathematicians." Jackie perked up when she heard "scientists." Science was one of her favorite subjects, but Miss Soraparu never called them scientists early in the morning. Science was in the afternoon. They

were never scientists in the morning unless they had a project due.

Jackie looked around. It was as if she was seeing the room for the first time. Every kid in the room except Alex had a folder on their desk. Some of the kids had presentation boards leaning against their chairs, and next to Miss Soraparu's desk there was a whole pile of posters and glittery signs. Their animal projects! Were they due today? She knew she had been a little off her game lately. The 75 on last week's spelling test proved that. But missing a whole project?! How did this happen? And it was no consolation that Alex didn't seem to have his, either. Alex never had anything.

"I know you're all anxious to get to share your new expertise with everyone, but we're going to split your presentations up over a few days so that we can get some other work done as well."

Some of the kids groaned, but Jackie felt a rush of hope. *Johnson is in the middle of the alphabet,* she thought. *If she splits us up over three days that*

at least gives me until tomorrow to put something together, even if she does reverse alphabetical order.

She'd stay up all night if she had to. Luckily, she had two blank poster boards in the art supplies in her room. She would have preferred one of those cool presentation boards that could stand up on their own, but to get one of those would mean involving her mother or father. The poster would have to do.

"Let's do this by classification, scientists." Miss Soraparu moved over to the board and wrote Kingdom Animalia at the top. "Everyone's animal should be in the animal kingdom, but I wonder what phyla everyone chose. If you can't remember your animal's classification off the top of your head, feel free to look at it in your report."

Everyone else flipped open their report folders. Even Alex took out a rumpled piece of looseleaf. Jackie was the only one with an empty desk.

"Raise your hand if your animal is in Platyhelminthes." No one moved.

"Tardigrade? Nematode? Rotifer?" Still no hands. Miss Soraparu smiled. "I can't say I'm surprised. What about Annelids?" A kid named Joshua raised his hand. Miss Soraparu wrote Annelids on the board, then put one tally mark next to it. "Cnidarian?" Angela raised her hand. "Echinoderm?" Julia put her hand up.

Miss Soraparu waited a moment. "Okay. What about mollusks?" Two kids raised their hands. Jackie didn't know what to do. She hadn't even chosen an animal. Elephants had been her first thought when they got the assignment, but it hadn't gone any further than that. Maybe she'd stick with elephants. She didn't recognize any of the phyla Miss Soraparu had said so far, but at least she knew that elephants were in phylum Chordata along with every other creature with a backbone.

"Chordates?" More than half the class put their hands up. Backbones were popular. Jackie quickly

put her hand up with the rest. She'd stick with the backbones.

"I assume the rest are arthropods because that's the only one left, but let's see a show of hands just to be sure." Five kids put their hands up, including Ashley.

Since there were so many chordates, Miss Soraparu read off the chordate classes as well.

Agnatha. Chondrichthyes. Osteichthyes. Amphibia. Reptilia.

On a whim, she put her hand up at Reptilia. Elephants were in Mammalia, but Jupiter was in Reptilia. She wasn't crazy enough to do a report on Jupiter, but draco lizards were pretty cool. She'd do it on dracos. Sam would be excited.

When all the tally marks were up, Miss Sorapu circled the groups. The arthropods and assorted others would present that day, the birds and mammals would present the next day, and all the other chordates, including the reptiles, would

present on Wednesday. That gave her two days to get her project done. She wondered if she could sneak her poster board into the pile by Miss Soraparu's desk without Miss Soraparu noticing.

But then Miss Soraparu added, "Pass your reports to your table captain. Table captains, put the reports on my desk. Neatly."

It was Jackie's week to be table captain. She pulled a random folder from her desk, collected report folders from the other three kids whose desks were pushed together with hers, and put her stack on Miss Soraparu's desk. She was careful to not be first or last so Miss Sorapu would take less notice.

With any luck, Miss Soraparu was collecting the folders for show and wouldn't actually check them before they made their presentation. She could always make some excuse at the last minute about having accidentally turned the wrong one in.

That did not work out in her favor.

When the class was headed to recess after lunch, Miss Soraparu pulled her out of the line. Jackie knew it must be a big deal. Teachers only got a break at lunch and the first half of recess, so if Miss Soraparu was coming to get her early, it must be important.

"Jacquelyn, I was going through the report folders at lunch. Everyone else's report is accounted for, and the only folder left is this folder of paper dolls. Is it yours?"

It was hers. There was no mistaking the yellow folder with constellations on the front that she had drawn by hand, but Jackie went through the show of opening it up to check anyway.

"I must have turned in the wrong one by mistake."

"I figured as much." Miss Soraparu smiled. "These things happen. Just run upstairs and put the right one on the stack. I'll be right behind you."

Jackie nodded and sprinted up the stairs. The only thing left was to really go all out "looking" for it,

then sadly declare she must have left it at home. She'd never been late on anything before. Miss Soraparu would definitely let her turn it in tomorrow, wouldn't she?

When Miss Soraparu made it to their classroom, Jackie had already taken everything out of her desk and was going through her backpack piece by piece. Ten minutes later Miss Soraparu hustled them both out of the door so she could be on time for recess duty. She was actually the one who suggested that Jackie must have left her report at home.

"Just bring it tomorrow. These things happen," Miss Soraparu said.

Tomorrow. The report required at least three books as sources, but between her bookshelf, Sam's bookshelf, and that old set of encyclopedias, there were probably enough books to do it at home without needing to take a special trip to the library. She could do this.

"Thank you, Miss Soraparu," she said, feeling almost as relieved as she sounded. "I'll bring it tomorrow." She had every intention to.

12
DRAGONS BREATHE FIRE

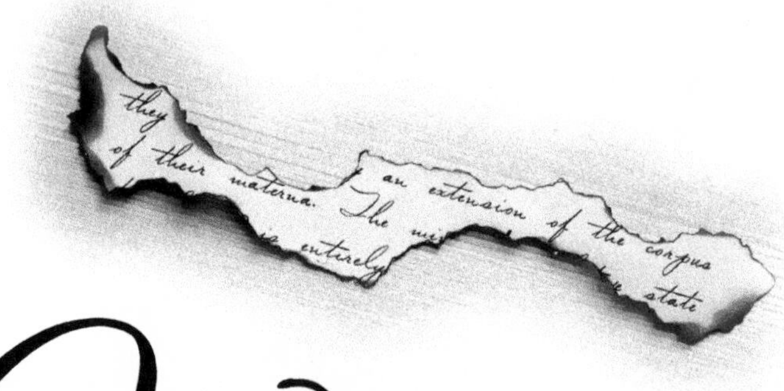

When Jackie got home, Jupiter was right where she had left him. She knew he wanted to fly, but she didn't have time to let him stretch his wings in her room. Right after school was the safest time to let Jupiter fly around inside. Her father wouldn't get home for a couple of hours, and Jacob, Jonah, and Judah were not allowed to go anywhere after school besides straight to the homework table. They weren't even allowed to go to the bathroom anymore. All they could do was

sit at the dining room table, take out their assignment books, and wait for further instruction. Their mother read each and every item written in their assignment books, and woe were they if one of them dared to leave theirs blank or—even worse—write "No Homework." Their mother would make up extra work for all three of them to do that was harder than anything their teachers would give them. You'd think Jacob would have figured that out by sixth grade, but apparently, he hadn't.

Technically John was not lumped in with the rest. Jackie and John had both proven themselves responsible about homework, so neither of them were required to go straight to the homework table. John did anyway. The way he saw it, Jacob already made fun of him enough, so there was no point in sticking out when you didn't have to.

Jackie didn't mind sticking out. She almost always went to her room first or made herself a little snack even if she wasn't hungry, just to show that she could. So those first few minutes every afternoon, Jackie would let Jupiter stretch his wings without

worrying about someone passing by. Sam was the only one who did. Kindergarten homework didn't take very long, so Sam was allowed to get something to read when he was done. Animal cards were strictly prohibited, so he brought his stack of old National Geographic magazines instead.

Sam poked his head in on the way to fetch his magazine and waved hopefully. Sometimes Jackie let him come in for a minute or two to watch Jupiter flying around.

"Where's Jup--"

Jackie shot him a look. Sam got quiet.

"I'm sorry," he said, whispering so loudly Jackie was sure her mother would ask her what Sam was sorry about. Mothers have great hearing.

"That's okay," Jackie said. It wasn't okay, but she let it slide. "We can do that later." She pointed to the terrarium in the corner. "Can you help me with something else, though?"

Sam nodded eagerly.

"Will you bring me your animal encyclopedia and anything you have on draco lizards? I'm doing a report on them."

Sam looked at Jupiter. Then he looked at Jackie. Then he grinned the biggest, most adorable grin possible, drew himself up to soldier stance, and saluted her. Jackie couldn't help smiling and saluting him right back. The kid really was a master of adorableness. It was a wonder he didn't get away with more stuff.

Between the real encyclopedias, Sam's animal encyclopedia, her animal encyclopedia, and two nature magazines, Jackie actually had a lot of material to sort through at the dining room table.

"Why the sudden interest in lizards?" Her mother asked.

"I'm doing a project. For science."

"Another science project?" This time her mother sounded skeptical. "Didn't you just have one of those a few weeks ago?"

"That was extra credit, Mama," Jackie said, hoping that her nervousness sounded more like busy-ness.

"And when is it due?"

"Next Friday," Jackie said. She couldn't say to-morrow. That would be too much like Jacob. "But we can bring in materials to work on our posters during free time tomorrow if we want. I think I might just do my poster tonight, though."

Mama nodded. "Get it out of the way. That's a good idea," she said, moving to go stir a pot in the kitchen while maintaining a hard stare at Jo-nah and Judah to stop them from doing whatever it was they were doing under the table. Probably silent foot wrestling. Their feet were usually pretty silent, but their faces gave them away.

Jackie felt good. She had two pages of notes, and she was only about halfway through her sources. She had a good excuse for lugging a project poster to school, she had at least fourteen hours left to work, and she had everything she needed to get done. She had been thinking she might have to stay up all night, but it was looking like she would probably be done by her usual bedtime.

She forgot to factor in dinner and watering the plants, but that still left twelve hours. No, two hours, actually. The report being due "next Friday," meant she didn't have a valid excuse to stay up late. If she got back up after her parents went to bed, she could get that back up to eight hours. Maybe ten if she could write under the covers with her flashlight while she waited for her parents to go to bed.

Ten hours. She could definitely finish her regular homework and pull together a report that looked like she had been working on it for weeks in ten hours. No problem.

After dinner, she went straight to work on her poster. Draco dussumieri, the southern flying lizard on Sam's animal card, was a dull brown color. That helped it blend in with the trees where it lived, but it didn't make it very interesting to draw. Draco volans, on the other hand, was. Now Jackie knew why Sam mistook Jupiter for a draco. He must have seen the picture of the draco volans in his animal encyclopedia before.

The draco volans was nowhere near as majestic as Jupiter was. Jupiter's wings were easily three times longer and looked like a stained-glass window in the right light. The draco's wings were colorful to be sure. She saw pictures of varieties with red, orange, blue, and green in their wings. To be fair, they were quite beautiful. But no matter how beautiful they were, the draco's gliding flaps would never be proper wings. Even if they could glide twenty feet, they would never fly. That was something she could give them. On her poster, she would make the draco fly.

She sketched a tree for it to jump from first, then spent a long time working on the lettering at the top before finally working on the creature itself. It took a few tries to find the right angle. She wanted to make it look like it was gliding graceful from the tree in the middle of a true flight. At first it looked like it was plummeting straight down, but eventually, she got it right with the body stretched out in profile and the wings tipped up slightly to show their full span. Once she was satisfied, she switched from ordinary pencil to color, and everything changed. With the first stroke of red Jackie could feel the draco coming to life. She could feel the current of air like a river, pushing it along. Holding it aloft. Higher and higher. The trees far behind. The trees far ahead.

Jackie worked, layering, coloring, bringing the draco's wings to life.

"Jaqueline Marie. Close my window."

Jackie looked up, startled to see her mother standing over her. She hadn't heard her coming in. She

hadn't heard anything. That happened to her sometimes when she was working really hard on something. It was like the rest of the world disappeared.

Jackie glanced at the window and said a silent prayer of thanksgiving that Jupiter was still out hunting. It was darker than she expected. Not fully dark, but late enough that she should have called Jupiter in by now and gotten herself ready for bed.

Her mother closed the window with a snap and locked the latch. "What are you thinking? The air conditioner is on."

"I'm sorry, Mama. I was trying to imagine what it feels like for the draco to glide on a breeze. I won't do it again."

"You better not." Her mother looked angry until she looked down at Jackie's poster. "Jacquelyn Marie, I believe you might be talented in the arts. This is beautiful."

Jackie blushed. It was beautiful. She had no idea how she had done it. She doubted she could do it again.

Her mother kissed her on the forehead. "Hurry up and take your turn in the bathroom so Jacob can go to bed at a decent hour. You can work on your project some more tomorrow."

Jackie splashed some water on her face and arms, tied her hair down, and raced back to her room to call Jupiter inside. As she opened her window, she could see him flying. He was circling high over Mrs. Albertine's house. From that distance, he easily passed for a bird, but she knew it was him. She stuck her hand out of the window and, without her saying a word, Jupiter turned to fly toward her just as a hawk swooped down to snatch him up. There was no time to panic. Everything happened so quickly. Jupiter angled his wings to the right, made a complete about-face, and unleashed a stream of blue flame at least as long as he was. The hawk shrieked as it fell to the ground.

Jackie wondered if that was what a shooting star looked like up close.

Somebody should have told the hawk that dragons breathe fire.

13
THE MORNING AFTER

The image of the fiery falcon played in Jackie's mind all night. It was horrifying. At least it should have been. There wasn't really a word for how she felt. It was like a roller coaster and a haunted house you didn't dare go into. Running to the top of the levee and barreling back down again or taming your first unicorn when you're young enough to still believe your whole imagination. It was flying, or at least how she imagined it.

Jackie had seen Jupiter breathe fire before. But she had never seen fire like that, never felt it like that. She was a jumble of feelings. Not one of them was fear.

When she closed her eyes, it felt like Jupiter. She could feel the wind holding her up. She could feel the disturbance in the air that even a noiseless shadow makes. And she could feel the power welling up within her as she turned to strike. Energy pulsed through her all the way to her fingertips. She couldn't have slept even if she wanted to.

For the rest of the night, when Jackie wasn't reliving the moment or wondering who would find the charred bird remains, she was writing. She was so glad that she picked the draco for her report. There was no way she could have given elephants any attention on a night like that.

It took her until first light to copy over the final draft. By then she was exhausted and exhilarated but mostly exhausted. The only thing that kept her awake was the memory of Jupiter. Jupiter Storm,

the defender, the slayer of evil. In the stories, he would have been enormous, big enough for her to ride on. As tiny as she was, Jupiter would never be able to carry her weight in real life. But life wasn't a story. And as glorious as it would have been to be with Jupiter on that amazing flight, she didn't want him to be any bigger. He was perfect.

Jackie's mind was full of daydreams when she arrived at school. She imagined being able to shrink down as small as a pixie and ride Jupiter without a saddle. Her mother had noticed how groggy she was and guessed that she had been up late working on her poster, but when she chided Jackie it was with a hint of pride, so Jackie knew she wasn't really in trouble.

Her poster was beautiful. Her report was finished and brilliant and on time. All she had to do was make it through a few short hours of school before she and Jupiter could be reunited. Then they would fly again.

When Jackie got to her classroom, she slipped her poster into the middle of the stack next to Miss Soraparu's desk, then fished in her backpack for her report folder. It wasn't there. She thought she remembered putting the report in her backpack, but either someone stole it, or she had left it at home. She wouldn't put something like that past Jonah, but when she thought about it, she couldn't think of when he would have done it. It must have been at home.

Miss Soraparu walked in with a cup of coffee and greeted Jackie with a smile. "Good morning. You're here early. You brought your report?"

She wasn't actually scheduled to present until the next day. It wasn't ideal, but Miss Soraparu would understand.

"I thought I did. I must have left it on my bed," she said.

Miss Soraparu's gorgeous smile faded.

"I was checking over it again this morning before we left. It's either on my bed or my desk. Can I bring it tomorrow?"

Miss Soraparu put down her cup of coffee and leaned forward so that she and Jackie were eye to eye. Miss Soraparu was only the fourth tallest person in the class, but she still had a long way to lean down. "I'm afraid not," she said. "Once is an accident. Twice is carelessness. I'm sorry. I can't accept it after today unless you have a written excuse. Otherwise, it wouldn't be fair to the other students."

"I have it. Really. I do. I just left it again."

Miss Soraparu smiled sadly but shook her head.

"Please?" Jackie was surprised to hear her own voice sounding so small. She could feel the tears welling up behind her eyes. She hated that.

Miss Soraparu brightened. "It's still early. You've got at least fifteen minutes before the bell rings. Why don't you go down to the office and see if you

can get your mother or father on the phone? Maybe one of them can drop the report off at school for you. Do you want to call them?"

And there it was. A perfectly viable solution staring her in the face. Either one of her parents would do that for her. Either one. But there had to be another way. Jackie hung her head in answer.

Miss Soraparu sighed. "I expect things like this from some of the other children, but I'm really surprised at you, Jackie. It's so unlike you."

Jackie didn't look up to see the expression on her face.

"Did you do it?"

Jackie's head jerked up. Until that point, she thought Miss Soraparu was talking about her forgetting the report at home. She didn't know she was questioning whether or not she had done it.

"I did do it!" she said indignantly. "I finished it over the weekend. I just forgot."

"Then why won't you call?"

"My dad's out of town, and my mom is too busy at work today." She couldn't say her mother was out of town. She was the one who picked them up.

Miss Soraparu looked exasperated. "It's your decision, Jackie. You can turn it in tomorrow with a note from your mother or father explaining its tardiness. Two days late, the highest grade you can get is an 80."

Jackie liked 100's, but an 80 was better than a zero. The only thing she had to figure out now was how to forge a note from her mother. No. Her mother had signed too many things and written too many notes for Jackie to pretend to be her. The note should be from her father.

After Miss Soraparu was done with her, the rest of the day slipped by in a fog. Kids did their reports. There was lunch. There must have been Math and Writing in there, too, but she didn't really notice.

She felt ill for most of the afternoon, but she always did when she was nervous.

At the end of the day, Jackie and her brothers all gathered at the kindergarten pick-up spot. It was a rule at school that siblings met at the youngest sibling's pick-up spot. Sam was chattering on about a picture of a pteranodon he drew when Jackie saw Miss Soraparu approaching. Miss Soraparu should have been in the fifth grade pick up spot with the other fifth grade teachers. What was she doing by the kindergartners?

Miss Soraparu didn't say anything, so Jackie just pretended she wasn't there. Their van pulled up. She and her brothers started moving toward it. It took her a few seconds to realize that her father was driving. Miss Soraparu shot Jackie a look, but went over to the driver window and spoke quietly with Jackie's father. Even if Jackie had been standing right next to them, she probably wouldn't have been able to hear what they were saying. Her father was a championship whisperer.

Miss Soraparu looked concerned, but she nodded and stepped away from the van by the time they had all finished piling in.

"It's not your day," Sam said after they pulled off.

"Yeah, Dad," said Jonah. "Why are you picking us up?"

Jackie's father glanced back at them in the rear-view mirror. "I'll tell you when we get home," he said, glancing back at them again. That time he caught Jackie's eye for a moment before saying, "Let's just get home."

14
THE FAMILY MEETING

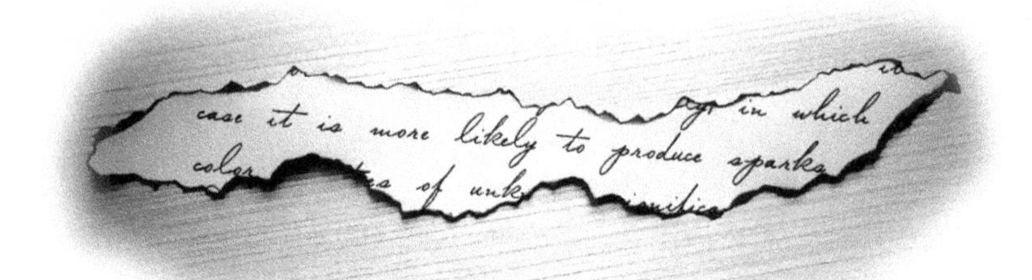

Everything was right, but everything was wrong. The house smelled the same. All the furniture was in the right place. The only thing that was off was her mother sitting at the dining room table. Her mother didn't sit. Not really. Especially not in the afternoon. There was so much work to be done in the afternoon. But as odd as it was to see her mother sitting oh-so-calmly at the dining room table, what was truly out of place was

the gumbo pot. It was sitting on top of Jackie's terrarium in the middle of the dining room table.

In a rush, Jackie knew why she was feeling so queasy. It wasn't the stupid report. It was Jupiter. Jupiter needed her.

Jackie rushed to the terrarium. Her father tried to hold her back, but he let her go when he felt how determined she was. Sam was right behind her, but when Jackie yanked the pot off the top of the terrarium, her mother grabbed Sam and pulled him away.

"It's just Jupiter, Mama. It's just Jupiter." He kept saying. "He's nice. He won't hurt you."

The gumbo pot was filled with rocks that Jackie dimly recognized as coming from the snapdrag-on pot. Who knew what the plant looked like, but she'd deal with that later. Jupiter was beating his wings frantically. As soon as she pulled the lid off, he flew to Jackie's shoulder and made a hiss-click-

ing sound aimed at her mother before threading his tail through her braid like he usually did.

Jackie's heart was racing. Should she run? Where would she go? The Jungle sprang to mind first, but that obviously wasn't a solution. If she ran further, where could she go? Who would take her in? Her uncle Michael lived in Hollygrove. That was close enough to get to on foot. She could hide Jupiter in his backyard and tell him...tell him what? There was nothing she could tell him. Nothing that wouldn't have him calling her parents to bring her right back where she was standing.

Suddenly being good at long division didn't seem like enough of a life skill.

Everyone in the room was staring at her. Except Sam. Sam was crying and still struggling to break free. "He's nice. He won't hurt you."

Jackie's father spoke first. His voice was calm. "Jackie? What's going on here? What is that thing?"

Jackie stood silent.

Sam spoke up. "He's not a thing, Daddy, he's a he." Her mother had loosened her grip and Sam managed to shrug free. "His name is Jupiter Storm, and he's a draco."

"That's a draco?" said Judah. "Cool!" He stepped forward to have a closer look, but his mother called him back.

"Judah, stop! All of you. Stay back from that thing."

"Mom!" Sam said, "He's not a thing, he's a draco."

"It's dangerous," she said.

John didn't move forward, but he did adjust his glasses and crane his neck a little to get a closer look. Jackie wasn't sure how much John could see from that distance. She assumed that Jupiter was mainly hidden away. He was small, and she had a lot of hair. But she had never seen herself with Jupiter on her shoulder except in the dim reflection in her bedroom window. She wondered what John saw.

"Dracos really aren't dangerous," John said. "Most lizards aren't."

Jackie looked at John and mustered as much of a smile as she could, which wasn't much. Maybe John had just given her the key. Sam thought that Jupiter was a draco. Sure, he was only five, but he practically lived in animal facts. If anyone would know an animal, it would be Sam. And if John believed, too...

"I don't know what that thing is," her mother cut in, all the educated polish peeling off her country girl accent, "besides the devil. Maybe the SPCA will know when they get here. Or maybe they won't."

"The SPCA!" Jackie shouted. "Mama, you can't!" There was no time to reason this out. No way to make it look better than it already did.

"Jacquelyn Marie, that thing is dangerous. I already called them. They're probably on their way. Now, I'm going to walk over to you slowly and start un-

braiding your hair where it's caught. Jacob, go fill up a bucket with water. Everybody else, back up."

"Mama, no! You don't understand. Jupiter is mine."

Jackie's mother looked at her, startled, then quickly regained her composure. Her voice smooth and steady as usual. "Don't worry, baby. It's not going to hurt you. I'm not going to let it."

Jacob returned with a mixing bowl of water from the kitchen. Her mother eased toward her and pulled the hair tie free from the end of Jackie's braid. Jupiter turned abruptly and hissed at her, but he didn't let go of Jackie's braid, and he didn't loose a stream of fire.

Jackie's eyes were burning. She could feel the tears welling up and rolling down her face in fat droplets.

"Mama, please. You have to listen to me." Jupiter had stopped making the hissing noise, but he pressed himself closer and closer to Jackie's neck as her mother unraveled the braid.

"I won't let him hurt you," her mother said. She was repeating it like a chant. Or a spell. "We've got water right here. I won't let him hurt you."

"Please, mama. I'll die." And as soon as she said it, she knew it was true. She was going to vomit. She couldn't let them take Jupiter. God knew what they would do to him. They would know the truth. They'd cut him open to see how he worked. They'd...They'd...

Her mother continued unraveling. She was more than halfway up Jackie's back. Jupiter's claws held tight like clinging vines. Jackie wanted nothing more than for Jupiter to run away. When her mother had loosened the braid all the way to her neck, Jupiter flapped his wings and flew to the top of the dining room curtains. Their house was old, and the ceilings were high—at least twelve feet.

Jackie's father nudged Jacob and said, "Take your brothers outside and get my ladder from the side of the house."

Jacob nodded and started to move.

Sam turned to Jackie, pleading. "Say it, Jackie. Say it."

Everyone froze and looked at Jackie. She stood in the middle of the room, hair half aloose, tears streaming down her face. They were all staring at her like she was some wild thing. Some skittish creature who needed to be tamed. Jacob should have been talking back, not dutifully ushering the children outside. All of it was all wrong. There had to be a way to fix it.

"Jackie, say it," Sam repeated as Jacob began to push him out of the door with the other Js close behind.

Sam was right. She had reacted too quickly before. She had run in wildly instead of thinking things through. She would show them. She would show them that she was in control.

Jackie stretched out her arm and raised her palm to the ceiling.

"Jupiter, come," she said. And of course, Jupiter came.

Jackie breathed in, and as she exhaled, she could feel herself calming. Her hands still shook, but it took the edge off the nausea.

Everyone in the room was frozen. Except Sam. Sam was trying to get to Jackie and Jupiter, but Jacob's arms were locked too tightly around him.

Jupiter wanted to fly free. He didn't struggle, but she could feel it as she put him back into the terrarium and placed the lid on it. No one moved until she put the pot of rocks back on top.

Jacob must have loosened his hold because Sam climbed onto one of the dining room chairs next to her and knelt there looking at Jupiter. Sam was whispering at Jupiter quietly which of course meant that the whole room could hear.

Their mother turned her attention to Jackie. "Jacquelyn Marie, I'm waiting."

What could she say? She couldn't think of anything. There were no magic words to turn back time and undo this whole thing. If there were, she would go back. She would go back and share him. She would let her mother see the chrysalegg growing. She would wake everyone the night Jupiter hatched. She still wouldn't have let the Js in her room, but maybe she could have devised a plan for supervised visits? But none of that was any use whatsoever. The SPCA was on its way. The only thing left was the truth.

So Jackie told the whole story, as much of it as she could. She left out the part about Jupiter's victory over the hawk. She figured that was too threatening for a first meeting. But she did tell them about the fire that first night. How Jupiter was born in a shower of sparks and the curling tendrils of flame that he made.

By the time she finished, her father and the Js were listening intently, as if it were story time and she was the teacher. Her mother was staring at the wall behind her.

"That's not what you said before," said Sam.

"I know," Jackie began, "I jus--"

"You said you got him for being good at science. You said Mr. Fowler didn't want him anymore."

Jackie wracked her mind for a way to fit Mr. Fowler into the story she had already told. She loved Sam and Sam loved Jupiter nearly as much as she did. She didn't want him to think she had lied to him.

"You said it was a draco."

"I never actually said it was a draco, you said--"

Sam kept talking. "It's not a draco. Dracos don't breathe fire."

They also don't have enormous wings or fly or come when you call them, she thought.

But what she said was, "I didn't know, Sam. I don't know what he is."

Sam was undeterred. "You knew he wasn't a draco, but you didn't tell me? I'm the lookout!"

"I didn't know." Jackie tried to hold his gaze. She reached out to hug him, to rub his hair like she did when he crept into her bed in the morning. He pulled back. "I don't know. He could be. I'm not some kind of draco expert."

"Yes, you are! You did a report!" he shrieked.

Sam turned his back to her, but at the mention of the report, her mother's eyes snapped back into focus. She pushed the report folder across the table toward Jackie. Had that been sitting there the whole time? It seemed as if it had appeared by magic.

"This report?" she said. It was an accusation, not a question.

Sam's silent tears turned into a full-on sob. He ran from the room. John went after him. Jackie wanted to go, too, but she couldn't. Sam would be okay. If anyone could calm him down, John could. He was a sweet kid. He would bounce back. She couldn't think about Sam, she had to think about Jupiter. He was lying almost lifelessly, either too exhausted or too forlorn to move.

Jackie turned to her mother. She didn't know what to say, but she needed to say something. Her mother cut her off before she could even begin.

"No. Not one word. I don't want to hear another word from you until this thing is out of my house."

"Vi," her father began, "don't you think we should hear what she has to say?"

"You didn't see it, Aaron. I did. Not another word until this thing is gone."

15
THE FIRST GOODBYE

They stood around well past dinner time, but the SPCA never came. At one point, Jackie's father stood up and said, "They're not coming, Vi," and started making sandwiches.

The Js started moving around, too. Jacob and the twins were messing around with a piece of lint or something from the floor. John eventually came out and announced that Sam was sleeping.

Jackie and her mother sat at the dining room table staring at each other. Jupiter was between them. Jackie wasn't hungry, but she knew Jupiter was. It was past his normal feeding time. She wondered how long he could survive without eating.

After a while, her father came and said something quietly in her mother's ear. Her mother grunted something like, "Fine," but she didn't look up at him, and she didn't get up.

Neither did Jackie. She stayed in her seat looking at Jupiter while things moved around in her peripheral vision. The Js came and went. Sam might have been one of them, but she wasn't sure. Her father moved back and forth a lot. Eventually, Jackie felt his large hand touch her softly on her back.

"Come on, Jackie," he whispered next to her ear. "Come on." And he gently pulled her from her seat, picked up the terrarium, and ushered her out of the door, leaving the pot full of rocks on the dining room table.

The next thing Jackie knew she was sitting in the front seat of the car her father drove to work and the two of them were barreling along the highway. She was aware of them crossing Lake Pontchartrain, but everything else was a blur. They might have stopped once, but if they did, she stayed in the car.

She could feel the car slowing down, but she didn't look up until she heard a strange man's voice.

"You just made it. I was about to close out early. You need a map?"

Her father nodded. They were next to a little guard house. A price sheet on one of the sliding windows had Tickfaw State Park printed in clear letters on top. The man pulled a folded map out of a stack by the window.

"The only site taken is twelve," he said, pointing to an area somewhere in the middle of the map. "Go ahead and take your pick of the others."

Jackie's father pulled out his wallet to pay, but the man waved him off.

"You can square up in the morning. Bathrooms and showers are over that way. Sure you don't need anything?"

"I think we have everything. Any one but twelve?"

"Any one but twelve. Office opens at 7:00."

The man lifted the gate arm, and with a final nod, her father drove through.

It was already dark, but it got much darker when they left the guard house area. It looked like they were driving through the middle of the woods on a path not really meant for cars, but Jackie's father seemed to know where he was going. They pulled off the main road onto a little area with a clearing. Jackie's father opened the back door and pulled the terrarium out from where he had wedged it on the floor behind the driver's seat. Jackie watched him. He put the terrarium in the

middle of the clearing, then went back to open Jackie's door and held out his hand to her.

"You coming?"

Jackie eyed her father's hand.

"Are we just going to leave him here?"

She thought he would say yes and, honestly, that wasn't the worst option. It was certainly better than the SPCA. Jackie didn't have any experience with the SPCA, but anything that called itself by letters was suspicious. If you didn't have anything to hide you could just say your whole name.

"No. I thought you could use a little room to breathe," he said. "Both of you."

It would feel good to move. She didn't know how long she had been cramped up. An hour? Three? She took her father's hand and let him pull her to her feet. When he shut the car door, the last bit of light in the area faded. It took her eyes a minute to adjust. By the time they did, she could see her fa-

ther squatting next to Jupiter's terrarium. He was looking at him. Really looking at him. When he saw Jackie approaching, he gave her a look that said, Is it alright if I open it? She nodded in response.

Jupiter didn't fly out immediately. She knew he wasn't dead. She would have felt it if he were. Still, she had a twinge of doubt when he didn't immediately fly to her. She had to put her hand inside for him to move at all. When she did, Jupiter climbed up only to curl up again in her palm. It felt good to have him there. She stroked the back of his head with her forefinger. When she stopped, he nudged her finger with the back of his head, the universal sign for "pet me again." She laughed and petted him again. He had never done that before.

Her father smiled a little, mostly with his eyes, and moved away to start unloading supplies from the car. He hadn't brought much. A tent. A couple of folding chairs. Sleeping bags. He set to work gathering kindling for a fire. The fireflies twinkled in the dark woods just beyond like constellations in the night sky. By the time her father had the fire

going, Jupiter was flying again, eating fireflies mid-flight. Jackie sat in one of the folding chairs and watched him, imagining that he was really eating starlight.

After a little while, Jackie's father settled into the chair next to her. He held a sandwich bag toward her, and she silently accepted it. Tuna wasn't her favorite, but it tasted good anyway. There were some strips of celery at the bottom of the bag, and she ate those, too. They were surprisingly satisfying. Her hair was loose on one side and braided on the other, which felt odd. She didn't know how to braid her own hair, so she pulled the hair tie off the remaining french braid and let it hang free. She'd regret it tomorrow when her hair was matted and tangled, but that was tomorrow.

She leaned back in her chair, as content as she could be given the circumstances. There were worse places to leave Jupiter. He seemed like he would be happy here. She guessed that was why her father picked this spot. There were so many trees. So many places to hide and sleep and hunt.

So much room to fly. He probably did belong there. She wondered if she could belong there, too.

By the time her father handed her a marshmallow on a stick, Jupiter had flown off again. She knew he was near even though she couldn't see him. She and her father were both roasting their marshmallows slowly, turning and turning them so that they browned evenly on all sides.

Without looking up from his marshmallow, Jackie's father said, "Do you think it'd be better for him to live out here?"

She knew that was where he was going, knew that was why he brought her here. Jupiter passed high overhead. She resisted the urge to call him back to her. She couldn't help remembering her mother's face when she had called him in the dining room.

"Seems to me he loves you, but he wants to be free."

Maybe her father was right, but she couldn't bring herself to say it. She just closed her eyes and tried to feel Jupiter flying. She wanted to say that he needed her. That he wouldn't be safe without her. But that wasn't exactly true, was it? The truth was that she needed him even though she wasn't exactly sure why.

Her father sighed and moved his marshmallow away from the fire. It was done anyway. "It's late," he said. "We can talk about it in the morning."

"No." Her voice felt strange. She hadn't spoken much for hours. "You're right. But can we stay a while longer?"

Her father gestured toward the tent. "We can stay until you're ready to leave or the food runs out. Whichever comes first."

Her father had brought plenty of food, so there was no danger of that happening immediately. They sat together enjoying the fire and eating marshmallows. Eventually, they got around to what hap-

pened that afternoon. Miss Soraparu had called her mother. Her mother had passed by the house to get Jackie's report and been somehow attacked by Jupiter in the process. Her father didn't know the specifics about the attack, but her mother had called him home from work to help her. He hadn't seen Jupiter breathe fire. He wasn't even sure it had happened until Jackie told her tale.

"I didn't mean for it to get so..."

"I know," he said. "We never do."

"If we leave Jupiter out here, can we come visit him sometimes? I mean, like, on the weekend?"

Her father nodded. "It's not that far. An hour and a half if the traffic isn't bad."

She had done so many things wrong. This was her chance to do something right.

"We don't have to stay until the food runs out, but can we stay until morning?"

He put an arm around her shoulders and hugged her in response. She just hoped that when she left him, Jupiter would know she didn't mean goodbye.

In the morning, Jackie's hair wasn't nearly as tangled as she thought it would be. Jupiter had slept in it all night, and at first light, he nudged her awake. She unzipped the tent and watched him fly away with her father's snoring adding to the morning music. Her father got up not long after her, though. He brought her slices of apples with peanut butter and a marshmallow on top. She ate them while Jupiter ate.

An early morning breeze stirred her hair, but when she closed her eyes, she could feel the air blowing through it more intensely. She didn't know if that was her imagining Jupiter's flight or that thing that happens when you close your eyes and everything else feels sharper and more real.

Her father didn't rush her. She sat for a long time wishing it could be like that forever. Her father had to go to work, though. And she had to go to school. She was missing her presentation, or at least she would be soon. Her father had said they could stay as long as she wanted, but maybe it was better if she didn't linger too long. They packed up the tent and cleared the site before the sun started to get warm. She thought it was early enough that she might still make it to school. Late, but not too late. Maybe they could say she had a doctor's appointment so her tardiness would be excused.

Jupiter swirled overhead like a ballet. She didn't call him back to her. He was too beautiful. Flying so high, his wings crystalline against the morning sky. He was powerful, and he was free. Maybe someday she would be, too.

Jackie breathed in deeply, and when she exhaled the breath was thicker, richer, more poignant, which was only natural. It was carrying the pain and regrets that are always packaged into goodbyes. She could almost feel that breath letting him

go, and when the last bit escaped her only remnants of the sorrow were left in her solar plexus. It was now or never.

"I'm ready, Daddy," she said. And the two of them quietly packed up their small camp. The last thing was the terrarium. Her father went to put it on the backseat, but Jackie stopped him. "We don't need it," she said.

Her father nodded, and before long they were driving down the little road toward the park entrance. Jackie knew that Jupiter was near, but she didn't look around to catch a glimpse of him between the trees. She kept her eyes on the road in front of her. When they got to the little guard house, the man from the night before greeted them. Jackie smiled when he said she looked like she was feeling much better and agreed that she did.

Jupiter was near them. He was hovering. She hadn't called the words or even thought them in her mind, but still, he was near. When they pulled

onto the main road that led back to the highway, he was still there. She wondered if Jupiter would follow them all the way back to New Orleans. No. Not follow them. Follow her. She and Jupiter were meant to be together. She didn't know how or why, but they were connected. She knew that, and apparently Jupiter knew it, too, because even when she set him free, he seemed determined to follow her.

Jackie closed her eyes and smiled. She loved it when Jupiter came at her call. She felt like a queen or fairy magic. But as tingly and wonderful as it was to command her dragon, having her dragon follow her without being bidden was even better.

The expanse of Lake Pontchartrain stretched out ahead. The lake was so big that it looked like an ocean. Even if you squinted, you couldn't see the other side until you were almost halfway across. Jackie had resisted looking for Jupiter until that point, but the idea of seeing him flying over the lake with the blue of the sky above him and the blue of the water below him overcame her, and

she scanned the skies. There were birds. Lots of birds. But no dragon. She could feel him there, just on the edges, but the further they drove over the causeway bridge, the fainter he became. He was staying. He stayed. The thought thudded in her mind. Was he afraid to cross the water? Was he trying to follow but couldn't keep up? Did he give up on her because she had given up on him?

No. That couldn't be. He couldn't think that. Not that of all things. She would never give up on him. He had to know. He had to know how much she loved him. But how could he? We don't abandon the things we love.

That's when she decided to call him. She whispered it, quietly. And when she could not feel him any closer, she did it again and again until her father had to turn to look at her and the tears streaked down her face. Then she was yelling and sobbing, her chest squeezing so tightly that she couldn't draw breath. It was as if someone were pulling out an actual piece of her. Something vital from deep inside her belly. She thought it couldn't

get worse until it did. The moment when Jupiter was gone—an absence, a feeling that had never been—she rolled her window down and retched with the car flying at highway speeds. She spat marshmallow and vomit, her father trying his best to tend to her while driving. There was nowhere to pull over.

Ten miles later they had reached the other side of the lake. Jackie was calmer. Or, if not exactly calm, quiet. She still called Jupiter over and again, but by then she knew it was useless and no longer wasted the breath. When they pulled up in front of her house, her father carried her inside like a baby and cleaned her face and hands. She was hot. Very hot. But that's what happens when one cries too loud for too long. She heard her father on the phone telling someone she had a fever. She just lay in the bed, smaller than she had ever been, wishing she could go back and make it all right.

16
PAPER DOLLS

Jackie was sick for three days. At first, her mother had blamed the marshmallows, but after the first day came and went and Jackie showed no sign of getting better, she began to suspect a virus and plied Jackie with juice and water. Her father suspected something different.

At one point, Jackie could hear the Js hovering around her door saying nonsensical things that she didn't have the energy to correct.

"Is Jackie gonna die?" That was Judah.

"Why would you say that, man?" That was Jacob. "You trying to jinx her?"

"I'm just saying what she said. She said she was gonna die."

"That was a figure of speech, dummy." Jacob, again.

"Yeah, Lieutenant Literal." Jonah always had to rub things in.

"I thought I was Captain Literal." Judah sounded confused.

"You got demoted."

She wished they would move away from her door, but she didn't tell them so. The only reason she bothered to listen at all was the small hope that Sam might be among them. He wasn't. Sam was the only one who could possibly know what she was going through. She just wanted him to curl up

next to her and fill the aching emptiness that filled her stomach, but he never came.

When she woke up on that third day, her mother was sitting on the bed next to her. She turned the damp towel on Jackie's forehead to the cool side and stroked Jackie's hair.

"If you're not feeling better today I'm going to take you to the hospital. This sickness is going on too long, Jacquelyn Marie."

Jackie's mother believed in giving your body a chance to fight sickness on its own. If her mother was talking about the hospital, Jackie thought she must be in pretty bad shape. Even in her daze, she liked the feeling of her mother worrying. Her mother's worry was a kind of assurance that she was loved, and knowing you are loved is one of the best feelings in the world. It cut through her fog and gave her a moment to think.

"Where's Sam?" Jackie asked.

Her mother smiled, a little relieved. Jackie hadn't spoken in days. "He's at school. He wanted to stay home, but I thought he should go back. He's been spending too much time sitting outside your door."

Now it was Jackie's turn to be relieved. She had so much she wanted to say, so much she wanted to ask, but it was like she was out of practice being herself and she didn't have enough words. All she could manage was, "I didn't hear him."

"He's been being quiet like you," her mother said. "Keeping secrets is hard on five-year-olds. Secrets and lies are hard on us all, but little ones especially."

Her mother was right, of course. She didn't have to say it all the way for Jackie to know it. Sam was too little to stand guard over a secret like that. That was why she had lied to protect him, right? There was nothing wrong with a lie if it kept everybody safe. Was there? All she knew was that she wanted to hold Sam close and squeeze him and

tell him she was sorry. She wasn't sure what else she could do, but she had to start somewhere.

"I'm going to bring you some soup. Let's see if you can keep it down."

The thought of soup actively turned her stomach, but she didn't say so. She just let her mother leave the room and closed her eyes to drift off to sleep. She dreamed the dream she had been dreaming since she got back. She dreamed she was on the ground watching Jupiter fly above her. She raced beneath him, trying to keep up until inevitably she came to a glass wall so high and smooth that she could never climb it. So wide that there was no getting around it. But this time, Sam was there. He offered to stand guard while she broke through. The offer was tempting. There were rocks and pick axes and other sharp things she had never seen before. She could do it if Sam would stand guard. The Jackie that was in the dream considered it, but then her true self took over.

Her true self asked her dream self, "What will happen to Sam? Ask him what will happen to him if you let him stand guard."

Her dream self didn't have to ask. She knew. That was the way it was in dreams. You knew things. If she went through that way, Sam would be thin as paper, always standing guard, never coming with her. Her dream self reached down to hug him. He was still solid and real and felt good in her arms. When she pulled back, Sam reached in his pocket and offered her an enormous pair of scissors. He meant for her to use them to break through the wall.

Jackie woke herself up before her dream self had a chance to react. She didn't need to see the next part. She knew what she needed to do. Her mother had left broth and crackers on the table next to her bed. Jackie tried to pull herself upright. Her arms were weak and shaky. The covers felt like weights. Her mother must have heard her struggling and came in to help her. Then when Jackie's hands trembled too much to keep broth on the

spoon, Jackie's mother fed her tiny sips one spoon at a time.

It wasn't so much that Jackie was feeling better as that she was feeling more determined. A third of the way into the soup she asked her mother if she would bring her her school bag.

"Don't worry about your homework now, baby. There'll be plenty of time to catch up when you get better," she said. But she brought Jackie her backpack anyway.

Jackie reached in and pulled out her yellow folder with the stars drawn on it. Mixed among the envelopes of paper clothes, paper animals, and paper circus gear was one labeled "Supplies." It contained a small pair of scissors, a few sheets of extra paper, and a tiny pencil sharpened on both ends. Her hands set to work feverishly, as if to ward off a spell. What kind of leader would she be if she left him behind to face the danger for her, fragile and defenseless? She would make herself out of paper before Sam ever could be. It

didn't matter what her dream self would choose. Her real self chose Sam.

Unlike most of the kids in her class, Jackie had never made a paper doll of herself. Her fantasies were enough fun that she didn't have to throw herself in the middle. But as she worked she could finally see the appeal. Her paper doll was free to adventure in a way that she never would be, not for years and years until she was grown up. When she added the finishing touches to her hair, hanging wild and loose to her waist, she noticed that her hands were steadier. When she began to fashion the stand, the ache in her stomach dulled. It was still there, but not as painful as it had been.

Jackie was feverish and tired, but when she stood her paper doll up for the first time, she felt like she had done something right. She felt almost complete.

Her mother kissed her on the forehead and went to clear away the paper doll things.

"Wait. One more." Her mother looked at her skeptically and made her take another sip of juice, but didn't take her things away. The next thing Jackie fashioned was Jupiter. She started to make him tiny and curled up so he could sit on her shoulder, but decided against it. There was no need for him to hide in the folder. She drew him with his wings outstretched in flight. That was when he was the most beautiful. The paper doll wasn't as splendid as he really was, but it didn't need to be. She would always see him truly in her imagination, and what would be more splendid than their both being free together?

Her mother made a face but didn't say anything. Last, Jackie added Sam. She drew him in a tiny captain's uniform with a dragon on the front. If he was captain of the dragon's guard, she and Jupiter would never leave him behind on their adventuring.

She felt better but not as good as she thought she would. There was still something missing.

As if in answer, Jupiter landed on her windowsill. He didn't look well.

"Mama, he's sick! Please!" Jackie shouted. It wasn't much of a shout, but it was more than she should have been able to muster.

Her mother hesitated for a moment but got up to open the window, pulling herself out of the way as Jupiter flew in.

Jupiter landed on Jackie's lap and nudged her hand with his head. As soon as he did, her mother flinched and started to edge around the perimeter of the room toward the door.

"Mama, don't," Jackie said. Her stomach was churning. Her heart was beating fast, and her body was suddenly flooded with the kind of energy you get right before you sing a solo. This was it. "Jupiter," she said, staring into his amber eyes, "I want you to be free." And she meant it. The truth washed over her in a wave. She had left him, but

she had never let him go. How could he ever be free if she never let him go?

Jupiter pulled himself up to his full height, stretched his wings and flew out of the open window. Jackie felt light, like she, too, could fly away on a warm current of air. She turned to her mother, smiling and suddenly ravenous. Her mother didn't look nervous. That's the thing about mothers. They may be sad or angry or scared, but there isn't a single one of them who can resist the joy of her child regaining health. There just isn't. So when Jackie smiled her true smile, her mother was so overcome with joy that she rushed in and hugged Jackie too tightly and told her that she loved her without once thinking to close the window.

Jackie didn't think of it, either. Jupiter was free. She could feel him soaring even then. He could go anywhere. It didn't occur to her that, of all the places in the wide world, he would choose to fly right back into her window. But he did, and it startled them both. Her mother jumped backward as if Jupiter were a venomous snake. Jupiter climbed

back onto Jackie's lap, never once taking his eyes off her mother.

Jupiter was feeling protective of Jackie. So was her mother. They just didn't know they were on the same team.

Jackie had taught her stuffed animals many lessons on manners. Being wild by nature, some of the lessons had had to be repeated many times before they stuck, including the lesson on making introductions.

"Mama," she addressed her mother first because she was the eldest and most important person to be introduced, "this is Jupiter Storm. He was born in a pot of snapdragons on the desk in my room while I watched. He eats insects and all sorts of pests, and he feels very protective of me." That was both formal and correct. She felt pleased. "Jupiter, this is my mother. She gave birth to me and loves me dearly and would do anything to protect me. Anything." Jupiter turned to look at her mother as if listening, so Jackie continued. "She was

born in the country but came to the city because she likes to watch the lights twinkle like stars. And I love her very much."

Jupiter bobbed his head in what might have been a bow, but might also have been him catching the movement of an insect on the floor. Jackie took it as a bow.

After a long moment, her mother said, "If he stays, he stays in your room."

Jackie smiled.

"And make sure you close that window at night. The air conditioning costs money."

"Yes, ma'am."

"And lock it when you're sleeping. And lock it when you leave. Any old body could come in here if you leave it open like that all the time."

"Yes, ma'am."

"And the first hint of something burnt and he's out of the house for good you, hear me? For good."

"Yes, Ma'am."

"And no more secrets, you hear me? None."

Jackie wanted to leap up and throw herself into her mother's arms, but after being sick for so long, she had to make do with a nod and a, "Yes, Ma'am."

"And, you." Her mother addressed Jupiter. "If you harm so much as a single hair on my daughter's head, I will box you up and bring you to the SPCA myself, and you won't be able to breathe enough fire to stop me."

Neither Jupiter nor Jackie took that as a threat. It was just the truth. And the only people who were threatened by the truth were liars.

17
LATER: AN EPILOGUE OF SORTS

Jackie didn't get well right away. It took a few days for her to regain her strength. Jupiter hardly left her while she did. Neither did her mother.

Eventually, Sam came in to see her. It took him longer than she would have hoped, but he came, and that was something. He was a little shy with her, but she knew he would come around. She just had to be patient with him. Five-year-olds have delicate feelings, and it wouldn't be much better when he was six. They played paper dolls,

and when Jupiter flew in, Jackie didn't stop Sam from petting him.

On Saturday, Jackie finally felt well enough to get dressed and eat at the table again. She wandered over to her window, expecting to see chaos in the front yard. She didn't. It looked lovely. The rows were less perfect than they had been and there were patches here and there where the grass was trampled, but it was still beautiful.

"Jacob, John, Jonah, and Judah took care of it for you," Sam said. Jackie turned to look at him. She hadn't heard him come in. "And Jupiter. John said he's one of the J's because his name starts with J, too. I guess that's why he helped."

Jackie smiled. Sam really was the best one.

They turned to head to the dining room. When Sam moved Jackie saw that behind him, on her desk, there was an old-fashioned paper parcel. The kind that's wrapped in brown paper and string.

"What's that?" Jackie asked. Sam turned to look.

"A present! Mrs. Albertine brought it for you while you were sleeping. She said Mama should do something to keep the birds from flying into your window." Here Sam tried to lower his voice. "She thinks Jupiter is a bird."

Jackie picked up the package, wondering if Mrs. Albertine could hear Sam's loud whisper from her front porch. The package was heavier than she expected. Jackie pulled one of the strings, and the whole thing opened up in one motion. Inside was a smooth gray stone and a postcard that said "Oregon" at the top. It wasn't signed, but there was something written on the back in neat, elegant handwriting. "Well done," it said.

This wasn't from Mrs. Albertine. It couldn't have been. *It was definitely from Great Aunt Mamie Seal*, Jackie thought. Perhaps the postman had just left it on the porch, and Mrs. Albertine had brought it inside when she came to visit.

There was a bit of parchment tucked in at the bottom. Jackie had never seen parchment before, but she knew what it was immediately. The parchment was folded very small. She could tell it was covered with writing, but the only part she could make out were the words "book" and "dragons" written in crooked cursive handwriting. Jackie wanted very much to pull it out and open it right then and there, but she left it cradled in the paper.

She would show it to Sam. Of course, she would.

Later.

About the Author

Marti Dumas is a mama who spends most of her time doing mama things. You know—feeding ducks in parks, constructing Halloween costumes, facilitating heated negotiations, reading aloud, throwing raw vegetables on a plate and calling it dinner, and shouting, "Watch out!" whenever there are dog piles on the walk to school.

Sometimes she writes, but only very occasionally and in the early morning.

For your own copy of Jackie's parchment, visit:

www.MartiDumasBooks.com/Jackie

(Of course, the original is kept quite out of reach in a library tucked in the side of a mountain, but the copy will do nicely.)

An Excerpt from Book Two: *The Dragon Keep*

1
THE TRAIN

Ten-year-old Jackie boarded a train in New Orleans with her dragon in a cat carrier. Her Great Aunt Mamie Seal assured her that, however uncomfortable her dragon was, he would be more so on a plane. Dragons cannot abide artificial flight.

Before an hour had passed, Jackie wished that she had put her little brother, Sam, in a cat carrier, too. He was all wiggles and bursts and his enormous stack of animal cards spilled into the aisle every six minutes like clockwork. That was to be expected when people, particularly little brothers, have just turned six, but despite Jackie's being ten and

more mature, her understanding of the six-year-old psyche did not stop her from being annoyed.

By contrast, her dragon, Jupiter Storm, was perfectly well-behaved. He was curled up on a cushion covered over in rocks and leaves. The cushion was more meant to keep the rocks and leaves in place than anything else. It wasn't for Jupiter's comfort. He preferred to ride on Jackie's shoulder, his tail intertwined in one of her long french braids.

Obviously, that wouldn't do on a train. Seeing him fly high up in the air was one thing. After all, people have a tendency to see what they think they see. A small dragon with wings outstretched in flight is a bird in the morning or a bat in the evening, even when he swooped down low to gobble up a tasty termite. Hardly worth a second glance. On a train, however, even the people-iest of people would eventually have to notice the way his eyes looked as if they understood, how his wings were proper wings, not flaps of skin for gliding, and how he, occasionally, breathed fire.

That last was still of at least some concern, moderate though it was. If Jupiter felt threatened, or if Jackie felt threatened--so much of it was one and the same--Jupiter might let loose a stream of fire as long as he was to keep them both safe. Jupiter was no more than six inches long, but six inches of fire can do quite a bit of damage if pointed in the right direction.

The best solution for this, of course, was for Jackie to remain calm. If Jackie remained calm and focused, Jupiter did, too, and the threat of curling tendrils of flame were reduced to practically nothing.

Jackie turned the clasp on her patent leather traveling purse, lavender to match her shoes, and reached in to touch the folded paper inside it for only the third time since boarding the train. She was careful with it. She had to be. It was a patchwork of parchment pieces lightly glued together and almost as thin as tissue paper. It was old and yellowed and covered in slanting black ink, but since Jackie had learned more than just how to

do her signature during her class' cursive writing unit, she could actually make out most of what it said.

She didn't dare pull the paper out. Not while Sam was awake. He didn't know about it yet, and she didn't want him to be upset that she'd been keeping secrets from him so soon after she'd promised not to. So, instead of pulling the paper out she mentally recited the parts she could by heart.

> *"Dragons of this variety who do not imprint on the human who seeded them, their materna, can, in some instances, imprint on an alternate human, although the connection will never be as strong. Unfulfilled minibus dragons, dragons with no materna or surrogate, seldom survive. The longest life of an unfulfilled minibus dragon on record is 17 days.*
>
> *Fulfilled minibus dragons cannot be tamed as they are technically an extension of the corpus of their materna. The minibus's relative state of wildness is entirely dependent on the proclivities of the human who seeded it."*

End quote.

Jackie didn't feel too badly keeping this secret from Sam. It was only a little secret, and now he knew

most of what the parchment said, even though he didn't know about the parchment itself.

Jackie turned the clasp of her purse back and placed it delicately at her feet.

"Aw!" Sam said, disappointed. "I thought you were getting a peppermint." He lowered his voice. "Or something for Jupiter."

He tried his best, but Sam was a terrible whisperer. Sometimes his whispers carried into the next room better than his normal voice. Jackie decided to distract him.

"Do you want to play the game?" Jackie asked. Sam nodded eagerly.

"Okay. Where's your map?" It turned out that Sam adored maps almost as much as he adored his animal cards, so a good game that involved sorting animals by traits and location on the map was enough to amuse him for at least an hour. Hopefully, Jackie playing along would stretch the game enough for them to at least make it out of Louisi-

ana without Sam telling the whole train car about Jackie's dragon. Fingers crossed.

Sam dug into his pocket and pulled out a large, folded map. The map was folded over so many times that the creases looked like bends, and he had to struggle a bit to get it out of his pocket. When he had, they did their best to smooth it between them. The route was already highlighted. Louisiana, Texas, New Mexico, Arizona, California, change trains in Los Angeles, then north to their stop in Klamath Falls, Oregon.

Jackie had never been to Oregon. In fact, neither she nor Sam had ever been any further than Texas. Just looking at the map was enough to make Jackie flush with adventure, even if she had not been on her way to learn to "take command of her dragon familiar." That's what Great Aunt Mamie Seal had called Jupiter: Jackie's dragon familiar. And no one contradicted her. It seemed no one ever contradicted Great Aunt Mamie Seal, and Jackie knew that she should try not to be the first.

Available March 2018

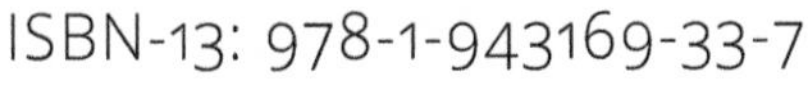

ISBN-13: 978-1-943169-33-7

CPSIA information can be obtained
at www.ICGtesting.com
Printed in the USA
LVHW03s2051250618
581820LV00004B/1189/P